Amanda's New Song

Amanda's New Song

Arlene J. Warner

Guardian BOOKS

Belleville, Ontario, Canada

Amanda's New Song

ISBN: 1-55306-165-9

For more information or to order additional copies, please contact:

Arlene J. Warner
505 Washington
LaCrosse, KS 67548
Tel: (785) 222-2651

Printed in Canada
by
Guardian
BOOKS

Amanda's New Song is dedicated to my husband Terry,
whose encouragement made this book possible,
and to my Friend, who gave me the desire to share it.

And He hath put a new song in my mouth,
even praise unto our God....
Psalms 40:3

1

A time to weep

(Ecclesiastes 3:4)

Amanda adjusted her seat belt, leaned back in the seat and closed her eyes as the plane lifted into the air. Her thoughts were chaotic, tumbling over each other, rushing to be paramount in her usually orderly mind. "You promised.... Where were you last night?—Amanda, I want a divorce.... No, no, we've gone through this before.... You promised never.... What about the children?"—*Lord, I can't go through this again.* She brushed her hand across her brow as if to wipe away all remembrance of the last two months and opened her eyes. *I will not look back; I am leaving nothing behind me*, she promised herself, silently.

"Lord, please help me, as You have so many times before; give me the courage and wisdom to accept the end of my marriage and to make a good life for my children," she prayed.

She stiffened her back and glanced at the little girl in the window seat beside her, touched her hand and smiled. The child smiled back and turned again to view the earth far below. *It's just like a vacation to her, she doesn't really understand*, thought Amanda.

"Mama, may we have something to drink?"

"Mama, may I sit by the window now?" The two little boys leaned over the backs of the seats in front of her vying for her attention.

"The flight attendant will be serving soon, Matthew. Joshua, you may change seats with Matthew in a half hour," she said, glancing at her watch.

Events of the past weeks forced themselves into her mind again. Shock: "Amanda, you probably don't want to stay here. Where do you want to go?" Trying to plan: take the civil service exam, better job—Colorado Springs, her brother lived there, near her parents. Separating lives into two piles: sell some things, write letters, pack everything, tickets, cat carrier.... "Yes, we'll take the cat. It will be one thing the children can cling to."

Now they were leaving the past behind and rushing to the unknown future at several hundred miles per hour. Time sped with them. The mountains below turned to the green and brown squares of the heart of America..

"What would you like to drink, ma'am?" The flight attendant's voice brought her back to the present.

She dawdled over her hot tea, and automatically ate the lunch set before her a while later. Then they were descending. Mountains again appeared in the distance.

She shepherded the children off the plane and onto a smaller one. They were on the last leg of their journey; closer and parallel to the mountains. In no time the plane began to lose altitude and the majestic Rocky Mountains were almost close enough to touch.

"It has been years since I saw this—I had forgotten how awesome they are!" she told the children. "The highest mountain over there is Pike's Peak. Remember, we read about Zebulon Pike." She thought, *How could anyone doubt God's power when they see His creation?*

"There are so many mountains, Mama," said Matthew.

"And they're all big," added Joshua.

"I see the biggest one, it's over there," said Elizabeth, pointing.

The plane circled as it descended and landed southeast of the city. *A beautiful place for a new beginning, a renewal—mental, emotional, and spiritual renewal,* Amanda said to herself.

It was a joyful reunion. Amanda hadn't seen her parents and her two younger sisters in over three years. She had never met her sister-in-law, Debbie, nor seen her two nieces.

The afternoon passed too quickly. Her parents had a five-hour drive to their farm and they spent some time packing the car with children's belongings—and the cat—and lingered over good-byes and promises to call at least once a week.. The children looked a little lost as the car moved down the street and Amanda's eyes filled with tears. *It's best this way, until I get settled. David's house is too small for all of us,* she thought. "I'll see you soon," she called aloud, and continued to wave until the car turned out of sight.

Debbie touched her arm. "Come in and sit down; I know you must be tired. Can I get you anything to drink?"

"No, thank you. I guess I am a little tired," replied Amanda.

A few days later, Amanda hung up the phone and smiled at her sister-in-law. "I have an interview tomorrow. Nothing from civil service yet, but this job sounds interesting."

Her days had been busy. She had rented a house in a good part of town: three bedrooms, one bath, a basement—her furniture would all fit. The utilities were turned on, except for a phone. She had found a small used car with David's help, nothing fancy, but low mileage and hopefully low maintenance. Perhaps she would have a job by tomorrow. The furniture van would arrive Monday.

The nights were the most difficult, when activity ceased and her thoughts ran rampant. *Divorcee. Divorcee.* The word seemed to echo in her head. A word she hated, a word accusing her, marking her as a failure. Finally, restless sleep would overtake her, and then another day to fill with more activity. Her prayers were disconnected. She hardly knew how or what to pray. She knew God had been close beside her since the nightmare began. She had felt His love and His guidance. He had brought her this far and she believed in her heart that He would always be there for her. Still, sometimes she would almost panic when reality hit her, like a blow to the stomach, and the thought of long weeks, months, years, trying to be mother and father, breadwinner, and homemaker made her physically ill. She would often fall asleep praying, "Abba, Father, please bring a man into my life—a husband for me, a father for the children. I don't want to be alone." She knew, though, that a woman with three young children was not likely to remarry.

That Saturday was spent celebrating her little niece Anne's fourth birthday. First, a visit to the zoo which was in the mountains high above the city. The little girls oohed and aahed over the baby lion and baby giraffe. Even the young camel was cute, they thought, but they hurried past the reptile house. By the time they arrived back at the parking lot, they were dragging their feet. At her house, Debbie brought out cake and ice cream and Anne's eyes gleamed in anticipation, while Sarah watched with ill-disguised envy. Presents followed and Amanda marveled at how good David was with the girls.

"It's hard to imagine you as a daddy. I mostly remember you in your terrible teens," she teased him. They reminisced, laughing at childhood escapades.

Suddenly, Amanda went to her brother and hugged him. "Thank you so much for letting me stay here, and for your love and support. You and Debbie have been wonderful and I appreciate it, little brother. I love you very much."

David gave her an embarrassed grin.

Monday morning Amanda started her new job. It was not very challenging but her co-workers seemed pleasant. It was an up-to-date office, her duties were varied, and it paid fairly well. Yes, she was ready to get on with her life. The moving van arrived and Debbie supervised the unloading of Amanda's earthly possessions into the rented house. After work Amanda picked up Debbie and some of her stuff from Debbie's house, bought a few groceries, and planned to put some order into the piles of furniture and cartons. She wanted to stay at her own place if feasible.

"The walls are a neutral color," said Debbie, "that's a blessing. You need curtains everywhere of course."

"I plan to make them," replied Amanda. "Maybe I can get started this weekend. Just simple drapes for now—a blue pattern in the living room, do you think? Maybe yellow in the kitchen. The boys like red and blue and Elizabeth probably wants pink again." She paused. "Maybe black in my room." She began to laugh and ended in tears.

Debbie gave her a hug. "It will be okay. Everything will work out. Come on, let's put the food away."

When Amanda opened the refrigerator door to put in the milk, she realized it was not cool. She checked the plug and the controls. Everything seemed all right.

"Debbie, the refrigerator isn't cooling."

"It's been plugged in since this morning; as soon as the men brought it into the kitchen. Do you think the plug is bad?"

Amanda plugged the cord into another outlet, but there was no reassuring hum from the motor. "I hope it wasn't damaged in the move. It's almost new. I have a service contract on it, so I'll call tomorrow. Could you be here for a serviceman to check it, Deb?" she asked. "I hate to ask—you've done so much already."

"Ssh, what's a sister-in-law for? I'll be here. Just let me know when," said Debbie.

Amanda gave her a hug. "Thanks, sister-in-law. Well, do you have room for this stuff in your refrigerator? And, by the way, may I stay with you one more night?"

"Oh, come on, you ninny, let's go fix some dinner before David calls for pizza."

Someone could check the refrigerator on Thursday, Amanda was told, and when Amanda arrived that afternoon, Debbie told her that the serviceman had spent almost two hours checking the refrigerator and could not find the problem.

"He said someone else would come out Saturday morning and try to fix it."

"Saturday! Oh dear, you may have a houseguest another weekend!"

"Good. David has to work Saturday, so after the serviceman leaves, we'll take the girls to the park or something," said Debbie.

That night Amanda ended her prayers: "Father, bless David and Debbie and the girls. Thank You for letting me come to them and get to know them. And bless Mama and Daddy for being there for me and taking the children this summer. Thank You so much for a family that loves me and gives me the support I need right now. Thank You, Jesus, for being my Friend. I feel Your love tonight. It surrounds me and makes me feel safe."

Amanda arrived at her house just before eight on Saturday morning. She walked around the front yard. She studied the nondescript gray stucco (in good condition), a few shrubs, a maple tree, an empty flower bed. She opened the side gate in the six-foot wooden fence that enclosed the back yard. Not much here—straggly grass, a couple of trees. The ground sloped up to the lot behind.

"Well, it won't take a lot of maintenance, at least." she murmured, "maybe I can get a few annuals for the front, and I can put the picnic table and benches back here. There's room for the children to play ball. It will do." All at once she felt a sense of anticipation. "It is going to be a new beginning." She walked to the other side of the house and unlocked the kitchen door. Her washer and dryer were in a nook to her right. There were storage cabinets above. The kitchen was L-shaped with walnut-stained cabinets and cream laminated tops, gray and white vinyl floor, sink to the left, electric range straight ahead, refrigerator to the right. An opening led into the dining area—windows on two sides, polished wood floor. Small, but the cushioned, black, wrought-iron chairs and wood-finish table, plus a small buffet were the only furniture, and they fit nicely. Off this was the living room—picture window on the left, the street side, and then the front door, the stereo in front of the window. On the far wall—a small wooden bookshelf, an upholstered chair and a side table. To the right—the couch, coffee table, and the hall leading to the bedrooms. Amanda surveyed this area critically. The couch was a bright blue smooth fabric, loose cushions, tables were black lacquer. This floor was also polished hardwood. The television set was to her immediate right. Cartons, some opened, others still taped, covered most of the rest of the area.

She searched for and found the coffee pot in one carton, and some mugs, plates, and bowls in another. *Where did I put the tableware?* she wondered. Before she could locate it, the serviceman arrived and Amanda led him to the kitchen. He pulled the refrigerator away from the wall and checked this and that with gauges and meters and then plugged it in. The motor purred. The man began to explain the problem (Amanda didn't understand a word of it) and said he would like to watch it for an hour or so until it went into defrost, to make sure it cycled properly. Amanda made coffee as they waited.

The serviceman asked her where she was from and she briefly explained that she was getting a divorce, had moved to Colorado from Maryland because she had family here. He told her his name, Rory, that he was originally from Texas (she could tell), that he had been in Vietnam, was discharged from the local Army base and had stayed on. He added that he was divorced and had one son who lived with his mother. They continued chatting over a second cup of coffee, and every few minutes Rory checked the refrigerator with his meters and gauges. He told her that this was his last day to work as a service technician. He would be starting an entirely different type of job on Monday.

Amanda was struck by his manners (that rare thing—a gentleman) and his humor.

The refrigerator continued to perform properly and Rory began packing up tools.

"You shouldn't have any more trouble," he told her. "If you do, call this number." He handed her a card. "As I said, I won't be there, but someone will come out and check it for you. Hope you like living here...." He hesitated.

"Thank you for spending the time to make sure it works," Amanda said, and held out her hand.

"My pleasure. Thanks for the coffee." He shook her hand, and stood there nervously. "Would you like to go to the driving range tomorrow afternoon?"

"Driving range? I'm not a very good golfer," Amanda stammered. "My clubs ... I don't know...." She gazed around her at the stacks of cartons. *Stop babbling!* she commanded herself, silently. *Just because it's been years since a man asked you out, don't act like an idiot.* She looked at Rory and thought there should be no harm in an afternoon date. He had treated her with respect. Should she?"

Rory looked at the floor, and reached for his toolbox.

"Well, yes, I would like that. My clubs are here somewhere." She smiled and pointed to the stacks of cartons.

Rory laughed. "Good, I'll pick you up about two, okay?"

She closed the door behind him and her good sense awoke. She sank into a chair in dismay. "What was I thinking? I've never done anything like this before. I know nothing about this man," she shouted at the empty walls.

She closed her eyes. "Abba, Father, if I'm being foolish, please forgive me and get me out of this."

Then she jumped to her feet. "It's too late to change my mind now, so get to work, Amanda," she scolded herself. She scrubbed the bathroom, the kitchen range and cabinets, and then tackled the mountain of boxes. She found the one marked albums and decided to unpack those first. She sat on the floor going through the collection.

Rachmaninoff, Tchaikovsky, Mozart, Beethoven, a few Broadway play soundtracks, perhaps a dozen jazz, several piano instrumentals, and a few popular including Frank Sinatra and Johnny Mathis. She chose one of Ella Fitzgerald's and put it on the stereo, thinking it should brighten her mood, and speed her unpacking. At 2:30 she remembered that Debbie and the girls would be there soon and hurried to take a quick bath. She was combing her hair when they arrived.

"So is the fridge working now?" asked Debbie.

"Take a look," replied Amanda. "Ice should be made by now—want some instant tea? Annie, Sarah? All I have is tea and water." The girls declined, preferring to explore the house and backyard.

Amanda set glasses of tea, well iced, on the table and sat across from Debbie.

"What was wrong with the refrigerator?" asked Debbie.

Amanda laughed. "I honestly have no idea! Something not cycling properly, I think." She lapsed into silence.

Debbie glanced at her, then grasped her hand and squeezed it. "This kitchen and dining area have great possibilities! What color do you want for the curtains—yellow did you say? Something bright to contrast with the dark wood cabinets?"

Amanda looked around the kitchen in a vague way. "Curtains ... yes, something colorful—a print perhaps ... red or yellow...." Her voice faded away.

"Amanda, what is it? Can you talk about it?"

"Oh, Debbie, I've done a stupid thing!" The events of the morning streamed out of her mouth. "And I actually made a date—a date, Debbie! With a perfect stranger. That's not like me at all. I still can't believe I did it."

"What is he like? You talked all that time, he must have made a good impression on you."

"Yes. He is nice, Debbie. He reminded me of an old-fashioned Southern gentleman. No, that sounds stuffy and he isn't stuffy; in fact, he jokes a lot. He's about my age, I think, divorced, has a little boy. He was in Vietnam and then stationed here—originally from Texas. He's nothing like the sophisticated, driven people I've been around lately. He's easy to talk to and he was actually interested in what I had to say, too. And he didn't make a pass. But, Debbie, I don't need any complications right now. I should have said no."

"Don't be silly! Go to the driving range and enjoy the afternoon. It's not a crime to laugh and have fun you know," she said gently.

"Of course, you're right. I'm making mountains out of mole hills."

"Right! I have to get home. Come for supper, hamburgers, remember?"

"I have to do a little shopping. I'll be over later to get the rest of my things. Thanks for listening to my raving...."

"Forget it. I'm glad you came here to live. I've wanted to get to know you. David has talked about you a lot, but you had been away so long, he didn't know you very well. Now we can really be friends. See you later."

Debbie called the girls and left and Amanda went shopping for cleaning supplies and perishable items. After putting her purchases away, she made a sandwich and went over her "to-do" list. "I'm a great list maker," she said under her breath, "organized me—in this area. Why isn't my personal life as simple to fix!" *Boring, boring,* came the answer from somewhere inside her. *Maybe I am boring—yes, I believe I am, but I wasn't always. I used to have fun. I enjoyed being a wife. I enjoy being a mother—it's what I dreamed of when I was a little girl. Dreams that now are shattered—divorce—that ugly word again. Divorcee—an even uglier word, and the words it conjures up are even worse—fair game, easy mark, not quite respectable, you know....* she could hear the voices of some acquaintances in her mind.

"Oh Jesus, I can't handle this! Please take me out of it!" Her head dropped into her cradled arms and she sobbed for several minutes. At last the sobs abated and peace covered her like a warm fleecy blanket.

"I never promised you a path free of stones, Amanda, I only promised to walk it with you," the words were clear in her mind. She answered: "I know, Lord. Thank You."

She washed her face, grabbed her purse and drove to David's house. He and Debbie helped her pack her few remaining belongings in the car. Amanda was exhausted and declined Debbie's invitation to stay for awhile. She kissed her nieces and left for home, where she unpacked the car, dropping the bags just inside the front door. She stood shaking her head at the disorder, then, being confident it would still be there in the morning, she went to bed. She was spent, emotionally and physically.

2

Call unto me, and I will answer thee

(Jeremiah 33:3)

Sunday morning, Amanda woke to a quietness in her spirit she hadn't known in months. She stretched, feeling refreshed, and planned her day as she started the coffee. First, call her parents and talk to the children, from Debbie's house or a phone booth. Debbie's would be easier, so she decided to wait until evening. She turned on the small radio on the counter, poured coffee into a favorite mug, sat down, and inhaled the aroma. *Ah, one good thing about New Orleans, I discovered coffee with chicory! Hope I can find it here.*

"Then sings my soul … how great Thou art!" She absently hummed along with the singing from the radio.

"I need to find a church. David and Debbie rarely go. Maybe there's one nearby. I'll check the phone book, *when* I get one…."

"For ye have not received the spirit of bondage again to fear; but ye have received the Spirit of adoption, whereby we cry, Abba, Father." The minister's voice caught her attention.

Yes, she thought, *fear is not of the Lord; I need not fear.*

"I shall never leave you nor forsake you," said the minister.

"Yes, Abba Father, thank You for that promise." She listened to the radio until the sermon was over—a sermon meant for her. Then she swallowed the last of the now cold coffee, straightened her 5'2" figure and tackled the largest carton in view.

"Oh, here you are!" Amanda pulled the golf bag from behind a stack of boxes. *The clubs are probably dusty, I haven't used them in years—never used them much. Face it, Amanda, you aren't a golfer, you're going to make a fool out of yourself this afternoon. Oh, well, I'll just have to make the best of it and then forget the whole thing.* "And, mutton-head," she admonished herself, "don't get into this kind of situation again." She lightly slapped herself on the cheek, and glanced at her watch—almost one o'clock.

There was a knock at the door just as Amanda was putting on her sneakers. "Well, here goes!" she said and wrinkled her nose at the reflection in the mirror on the door—a small figure, too short, nose a little long, softly curling, medium-length dark hair, a mouth—never mind the mouth, rather fine dark eyes—her best feature. White slacks, pink patterned shirt and white shoes completed the image.

"Hi! I was afraid you weren't going to answer—had changed your mind. I'm glad you didn't," Rory said when she opened the door.

"Come in. I almost did … change my mind—I'm no good at golf," she said as she picked up her clubs. "I really haven't played in years," she added when they were in the car. "You are welcome to pretend you've never seen me before, if you like," she joked nervously.

"You'll be fine—like riding a bicycle I think—you never forget."

She stole a glance at him as they drove away. He's very attractive—blond hair, not long as so many men wore it these days; blue-green eyes (she wasn't quite sure), not too tall, capable, deep chest (she always noticed a man's chest), strong hands and arms, wide shoulders, not hidden by his yellow short-sleeved sport shirt, a friendly, easy manner, good sense of humor. His car didn't seem to fit him—a light green station wagon a few years old, but clean and polished.

The driving range was on higher ground on the northeast side of the city. It faced the mountains and Amanda would rather have looked at the view than the ball. She had wanted to watch Rory for awhile, hoping it would help her remember what to do, but he had handed her a club, placed her ball and stood waiting for her to take a swing. She bit her lip, set her feet, bent her knees, drew back the club and swung. The ball sailed out about ten feet, bounced and rolled to the left. Amanda was surprised she had even hit it.

"Hit another ball while I watch your swing," Rory said.

Amanda took a deep breath, and trying to keep her eye on the ball, swung. This time the ball traveled twenty yards or so, most of it to the left.

"Hmm, try this." Rory stood behind Amanda and guided her through the sequence of stance, swing, follow-through. It didn't seem to help much. Amanda persuaded Rory to go ahead with his practicing, and she would try to figure out what she was doing wrong. She watched him hit several balls straight and long and wished she was anywhere but in this beautiful place, on this beautiful day with a club in her hands and a bucket of balls beside her. She had played several times, and while she had not played very well, she had thought she would remember something! She determined to work at it and placed another ball.

Her concentration was broken when Rory asked if she would like another bucket of balls. She looked up. He was standing behind her, swinging his empty bucket. She shook her head and pointed to hers which was over half full. He waved and left. When he came back, he tried to help her and she finally did make a few respectable drives. The range was almost empty. (Amanda was profoundly grateful for that.) Most golfers were on the course on such a fine day. Amanda relaxed and decided to make this fun if it killed her, and time passed with friendly banter and soft laughter (and little improvement in either one's golf game). The sun was shining in their eyes as it sank toward the mountains and they laughingly gave it up.

Amanda breathed a sigh of relief as she leaned back against the car seat. At last it was over. *Although*, she smiled to herself, *it was rather fun toward the last. Well, I've had my big date and now I can concentrate on my job and getting the house in order, and my refrigerator is fixed, too!*

"Would you like a cup of coffee, or iced tea?" Amanda asked politely, as they got out of the car. She thought that she owed him that much for putting up with her.

Rory placed her golf bag against the wall next to her door, "I wish I could, but I start that new job in the morning and I have to get some things ready. I worked most of yesterday, you know." He winked at her. "Would you have dinner with me tomorrow night?"

"I-I can't, really. I must do something with all those boxes in...."

"How about Tuesday night?"

"Tuesday, I ... all right, Tuesday will be fine."

"Great! Seven o'clock okay?"

"Seven, yes. Thank you for the afternoon. It was fun." She smiled at him.

"I had fun, too. I'm really glad you came. Can I call you tomorrow after work?"

"Oh no, you can't—I mean my phone is supposed to be connected sometime next week."

"Until Tuesday, then." He took both her hands in his, squeezed them and turned down the walk.

Amanda, her face flushed, fumbled for her key, jabbed it into the lock and snatched up the golf bag. Inside, she shoved the door shut with her foot, dropped her purse and clubs on the floor and covered her face with her hands.

"What an idiot you are, Amanda," she said to herself. "You acted like a teenager." She sank to the floor. "I don't know what to do, what to say, how to act on a date. Tongue-tied, babbling—oh how embarrassing! I can't believe he asked me out again." She sat there a few minutes going over their conversation in her mind and began to smile, then to laugh. She scrambled to her feet, grabbed her clubs and walked toward the closet. "A femme fatale you are not, Amanda!" she said, giggling.

She decided to call the children from the supermarket rather than driving the several miles to David's. To be honest, she simply didn't want to tell Debbie about the afternoon.

She would try to keep the call short, as she didn't have much change. Catherine answered and told her everyone was doing well—the children didn't seem to be overly bothered by being with virtual strangers. Amanda told her that she had a job and was making curtains for the house. She spoke to each child for a few minutes, stressing her love and telling them she was proud of them. She hung up knowing they were in good hands, yet dissatisfied with long distance hugs and mere seconds to listen to their little voices. Tears slid down her face as she drove home.

Activity was the best antidote she knew for the blues, so she started doing laundry. Then she washed an apple and put it in her purse for tomorrow's lunch, heated water for tea, and stuck a stalk of celery and a few saltines on a plate for her supper. She stared at the cartons for a minute or so, while munching on celery, then forced herself to strip off the packing tape on one marked "Bath." Easy enough—within a few minutes, towels and wash cloths were stacked neatly in the hall closet. She unpacked three more cartons—most contained kitchen items, which she placed on the counter to wash later. She nibbled and sipped as she worked, and was amazed when she noticed her watch said 10:30. She fell into bed, tired and disheartened. Her prayers were uttered more from habit than fervor and her pillow was damp with tears when she finally fell asleep.

Tuesday, Rory knocked on her door promptly at seven. Amanda

was startled at the way her heart pounded and her pulse raced, but she admitted him with a cool smile. He apparently noticed nothing untoward, and ushered her to his car. She listened perfunctorily as he chatted about his day. She was still shaken from the powerful emotions that had swept over her at Rory's knock. How strange, how unsettling. She willed herself to relax and by the time the car stopped, her self-control was in its usual place.

Rory had chosen a Chinese restaurant that resembled a pink pagoda, located on the south side of the city. Amanda was amazed at her appetite. Chinese cuisine was a favorite and the food flavored with the sound of the waiters conversing in their native tongue produced an entrancing atmosphere. Rory kept the conversation going, employing several topics and relating jokes he had heard, and she found herself having a good time. They laughed as they read the predictions in their fortune cookies.

As they walked to the car, Rory suggested a drive into the foothills, and Amanda agreed without hesitation. Then realizing what she had done, she came to a sudden stop.

"What's wrong?" asked Rory, who was holding her arm and necessarily stopped with her.

"I … uh … something in my shoe, I think." She held his arm as she took off one high heel and shook it vigorously before putting it back on her foot.

Rory took a winding road to an overlook high above the city. The view was spectacular. Streetlights, house lights, and car lights, interspersed with colored traffic lights spilled out for miles in all directions. They left the car and leaned against the retaining wall.

"How beautiful!" said Amanda, and breathed deeply. "It's so tranquil up here and it smells heavenly."

"Pines," said Rory.

"'Look for a lovely thing and you will find it, it is not far,'"[1] quoted Amanda.

Rory looked at her, surprised. "Who said that?" he asked .

"I'm not sure, Sara Teasdale, I think."

They stood in the cool of the evening, too enthralled to speak. The lights below were echoed in the sky above by myriads of stars. The silence was companionable, not awkward. Time passed, and at last Amanda glanced at her watch, and sighed with regret. She touched Rory's arm. "I must go. It's getting late."

"Yes, I guess it is," he agreed. He took her arm and handed her into the car.

The quietness continued as they started down the mountainside; both apparently still savoring the moments they had shared without words. When Rory reached for Amanda's hand, she did not pull away.

"I enjoyed this evening very much,"she told him. "I was almost dreading it, not knowing what to expect—on a date—I guess I was afraid. You're so different from the men I've known."

"Oh, how do you mean?"

"I'm not sure I can explain. I feel comfortable with you. I don't have to be on guard all the time, or prove anything, or feel I have to keep you entertained. It's all so natural somehow. You're what I call a gentleman. That's meant to be a compliment. I guess it's an odd thing to say these days, but—I'm putting it very badly—but I feel safe and secure with you, and at the same time I feel happy, and ... well, you make me smile."

She stopped and looked toward him. She could see his face only dimly by the flickering lights as the car moved on the city street. He didn't appear to be listening to her.

"That was silly. I'm sorry; forget what I said." She lapsed into silence, not understanding his mood.

To her surprise, Rory suddenly pulled into a dark parking lot and turned off the engine. He turned to look at Amanda.

"This evening was very special to me. I haven't enjoyed myself this much in a long, long time. You're not like the girls I've known either. There's something different about you—you're so little, but … the way you carry yourself, you seem taller. I think dignity is the word I'm looking for to describe you. And I like to listen to you talk. It isn't nonsense, it has meaning." He continued to study her. "You're a very sweet person, Amanda." He leaned toward her and kissed the tip of her nose, then her lips. Amanda's pulse quickened as she responded.

"I must get you home," said Rory, as he gently released her and started the car. No words were spoken.

At her door, he said, "I'm tied up tomorrow night. Is your phone in yet?"

"No …" began Amanda.

"So I can't call you. I'll be by early Friday evening. Decide where you'd like to go." He bent and kissed her lightly. "Good night, Little One," and he was gone.

As Amanda got ready for bed, her actions were automatic, her thoughts confused. As usual, she turned to God before going to sleep. She liked to go over her day with Him, thanking Him for blessings, asking for forgiveness, asking for strength. And praising her one true Friend, who never let her down. "What is happening, Father? You know I asked You to bring a man into my life, for me and for the children. But it's too soon, isn't it? I don't think I'm ready. I do thank You for this day, though, and this evening. It was fun after I got over being so nervous. Thank You, Jesus.…" She fell asleep murmuring praises.

3

Ask, and it shall be given you

(Matthew 7:7)

The next two days went quickly. Amanda was becoming comfortable with her job. Her duties were not difficult and she handled them with ease. On Thursday her phone was at last installed and that night she called her parents and spoke with each of the children. They were enjoying the novelty of the farm and were learning new skills under the tutelage of Amanda's young sisters, as well as their grandparents. Amanda's mother suggested that the children stay all summer as it would be more fun for them. "You wouldn't have to find a sitter." The children agreed with their grandmother and Amanda promised to think about it. She told them she would drive down to visit in two weeks. She gave and received kisses over the phone and hung up feeling lonely. She realized that it would be better for the children to stay with her parents for the summer, but she missed them terribly. I'll think about it and pray about it, she decided.

Friday was not a good day at work. Amanda's boss cornered here in the supply room. He had made several lewd comments to her during the week. She had thought her disapproving words had been sufficient to discourage him for good. He was not her immediate boss, actually he was the owner, and old enough to be her father. In all the years of working, she had been forced to handle such harassment only twice. But now he came into the supply room behind her, stretched his arms across the aisle between the shelves and she could not escape. He proceeded to comment on her being lonely and how she needed someone to take care of her and he would be happy to oblige.

I have to stop this now, she thought, *or leave this job.* She prayed a quick prayer asking the Lord to help her say the words that would squelch this man for all time, and, *If possible, Father, please let me keep my job.*

She drew a deep breath. "Sir, you are mistaken if you think your ugly comments are complimentary. I doubt you realize how much they offend me. I would like to continue working here, but it must be on a strictly business basis, without any chance of this happening again. Believe me, I am not interested in *anything* else."

His leer vanished and his arms dropped to his sides. He muttered that he didn't know what she was talking about; that he was simply looking for refills for his desk pen, turned and left, leaving the door open.

Amanda leaned against a shelf. "I wonder what happens now," she whispered to herself as she picked up her supplies and went back to her office. The receptionist told her that the boss had left and would not be back today. At five she gratefully locked her desk and walked to her car. The beauty of her surroundings held her in awe for a minute or so. The sun was setting behind the peaks only a few miles away. A light breeze filtered through her hair. This is a lovely place to live—a peaceful place. The children and I will make a good life here. She lifted her head, stuck out her chin, and climbed into the car. As she drove, she purposely put the earlier unpleasantness out of her mind.

Rory arrived about six. He admired all the progress Amanda had made in the house.

"I thought I would help you this evening, unless you had something special you wanted to do. Is that okay?" he asked.

Amanda was surprised and delighted, and she cheerfully accepted his offer. First, he put a record on the stereo—Tchaikovsky's *Nutcracker Suite.*

"It's not Christmas," she protested.

"I like it anytime of year," he insisted. He carried boxes to the designated rooms, broke emptied ones down and stacked them in the garage, saying he would dispose of them when they were finished. He stacked books on shelves (alphabetically according to author as she requested) and dried the china she washed.

"You're amazing," she told him. "Do you cook too?"

"Army," he said, with a grin. "I can cook a little."

"I'm not used to having someone help me around the house," she admitted.

When only a few boxes remained—odds and ends that Amanda wasn't sure what to do with—she called a halt. She poured strong coffee that had been brewing all evening.

"This is pretty potent stuff, are you sure you want some?"

"It is strong," he admitted, after a sip or two. "What kind of coffee do you use?"

"It has chicory in it. I learned to like it when I lived in New Orleans. Some people don't care for it."

"It takes a little getting used to, but I like it … I think!" He grinned and took another sip. "Are you hungry?"

"My goodness! I didn't think. I sometimes don't eat at night. Would you like a sandwich, soup, maybe a salad, or how about an omelet?"

Rory chopped onions and tomatoes while Amanda grated cheese and beat the eggs. She made toast and started fresh coffee. They sat in the kitchen enjoying the food and each other's company.

"I noticed one bedroom has no bed in it," Rory commented.

"Yes, that's Matthew and Joshua's room. I sold my bedroom set and decided to take theirs for myself. I have to buy a bed before I bring them home."

"I have one you can use if you want it. Some friends moved and gave me two extra beds, among other things."

"I don't know … I wouldn't want to…."

"It's just stored away. Someone should get some use out of it. It's yours if you want it. I could bring it over tomorrow."

"Well, if you're sure. That would be great—one thing I don't have to buy. No hurry though. The children will stay at my parent's all summer, I think."

"What are you doing tomorrow?" Rory asked.

"Shopping with Debbie in the morning. I need clothes for work and material for curtains. I hope to get the living room ones finished tomorrow."

"I can't do much to help you with that, but I could mow the lawn. I saw the mower in the garage, and there's a gas can."

"You don't need to do that! I can mow…."

"I'm sure you can," he agreed, "but I would like to do it if you'll let me."

Amanda smiled at him. "I would be stupid to say no, if you're sure…."

"I'll be here early afternoon. I heard about a dinner and dancing place. Would you like to go tomorrow night? I'm told the food and music are good. Do you like to dance?"

"Yes, I love dancing, but I haven't danced in a long time. I probably don't know the new steps."

"We'll learn together," he promised.

Rory left after kissing Amanda sweetly at the door. Amanda took a quick bath and climbed into bed. She fell asleep, as she so often did, talking to her Friend about her day.

4

A time to laugh

(Ecclesiastes 3:4)

Saturday morning Debbie took Amanda shopping. Her wardrobe had consisted mainly of slacks and shirts, with a couple of tailored dresses for church. She had made do with that at work the past two weeks. They had a pleasant time shopping and Amanda bought three work dresses and material for living room and kitchen/dining curtains. She arrived back at the house about noon and began working on the curtains: preshrink, dry, cut, sew. Rory arrived about two and waved at her from the drive when she opened the door. She went back to her curtains, smiling as she listened to the mower go back and forth across the front lawn. About five Rory knocked, said he was finished, the water sprinkler was going, and that he would be back in a couple of hours. The curtains were ready for pressing and hanging, and Amanda put everything away.

Amanda began dressing, taking extra care with her make-up, using more color than usual. Every twenty minutes or so, she would slip on a cotton housecoat and run out to move the sprinkler. She chose a two-piece dress of soft yellow that was several years old but had been worn little and was still in style. She pinned a cameo encircled with gold filigree on the front of her dress and fastened small dangling gold earrings in her ears. She had slipped into white high heeled sandals and picked up a white crocheted shawl to drape around her shoulders when Rory arrived about seven. His mouth pursed, stopping just short of a whistle, at the onset of a frown on her face, and he gave her a big smile instead. He was jauntily dressed in dark slacks, a gray-patterned jacket and a striped tie. Amanda's face underwent an alteration, and she smiled back. She felt young and carefree as they drove away.

They ate steak—his rare, her's medium—and danced for hours. Rory was a good dancer. He held Amanda very close during the slow pieces and she felt at ease in his arms, as though she belonged there. She found herself enjoying the faster music as well and tried to match his steps.

It was very late when Rory kissed her lingeringly at her door. She had no thought of pulling away.

"How about a drive in the mountains tomorrow?" he asked as he unlocked her door for her.

"I think maybe we have seen enough of each other for a couple of days, don't you? I think we should…."

"No, I don't think we should. Amanda, I enjoy being with you. I want to spend more time with you, not less. How do you feel about that?"

"I enjoy being with you, too. I just think we're…." The look in his eyes stopped her.

"Amanda…."

"I must go in," Amanda interrupted. "I'd like to go to the mountains tomorrow afternoon. Good night, Rory, I had a wonderful evening."

She wrenched the door open and went inside. She stood quietly with her back to the door, hardly daring to breathe. After a few moments, she heard footsteps on the walk and the sound of an engine.

She took a deep breath and collapsed on the couch. Her heart was pounding. *What is happening? I've only known Rory a week—one week!. Yet I feel as though we're old friends—that we've known each other almost forever. I like him. I like being with him, very much. I tried not to.* She sat up. *How could I fall for the first man I meet! He doesn't try to take advantage of me, even though he must know how vulnerable I am right now. He seems to know, to really care. I think he's lonely, too. Oh, Amanda, you must be careful—very, very careful.*

Sunday morning Amanda went to a nearby church. She hated going alone, but she needed to find one that would suit her and the children when they came home. The people were friendly and the minister spoke well and had a good message. The church was large, modern, and only a few years old. The sanctuary was beautiful. She did not know if this would be her church home or not, but she came away with the peace that comes with worshiping God.

She spent the early afternoon hanging curtains. They looked pretty good she thought; at least they would do for now. The bedrooms would continue with sheets on the windows until next month. Suddenly she realized how late it was. She ate cheese and crackers and a banana while adding to her shopping list, took a quick shower, and had just finished dressing when Rory knocked on the door.

He accepted her offer of coffee and sat on the couch. "You've made a lot of progress this week. This room is very comfortable now," he told her as she returned with two steaming mugs. "And you look very pretty. Ready to go?"

They traveled west up the pass. Towering pine-covered mountains dwarfed the highway. Amanda had to bend her head low to see the mountaintops from inside the car. It was breathtaking and reminded her of pictures she had seen of the Alps. Now and then she spotted a house perched on the mountainside, almost hidden by the trees. She could see no road and wondered how they got vehicles up there, especially in winter.

The air was much cooler at this altitude and Amanda drew it in in gulps, savoring its freshness. She knew Rory was amused by the grin he was trying unsuccessfully to hide, but she didn't mind. She wanted to take in this beauty until she was filled.

Rory reached over and patted her knee. "I'm glad I brought you here. I like to watch your face when you're enjoying yourself. There's a sparkle in your eyes."

I misjudged him, I won't make that mistake again, she thought and smiled at him. "I thank you for bringing me. It's so … actually, I'm speechless," she admitted.

At a small town, they turned south on a narrow, winding road. At one point, they had to stop at the entrance of a one-way tunnel to allow a car through from the opposite direction. They continued to climb, but at a lesser grade. On either side of the road were meadows with cattle grazing contentedly, or lazily drinking from small streams, or running, seemingly without purpose. Still higher peaks rose in the distance. Wild flowers of white, yellow, and lavender softened the dark rocks that were strewn over the land, as if they had been carelessly dropped by a giant hand.

Rory told her stories of gold mining days and pointed out the remains of several old mines clinging precariously to slopes.

"You know quite a lot about the area. How long have you lived here?" she asked.

"About three years. I was stationed here after Vietnam and stayed after my discharge."

He told her about growing up in East Texas, about working in Huntsville, Alabama, with his father on the space program but very little about the war, except that he had been a diesel mechanic—working on tanks and other heavy equipment. He had married before going into the army, had a son three years old, and had been divorced two years.

She told him of her marriage while her husband was in college, three babies in two-and-a-half years, about other women in his life, separations, reconciliations, living in seven states in thirteen years, and finally her husband asking for a divorce about three months ago.

"How did you decide to come here?" he asked.

"I wanted to be close to family. My brother is here and my parents not too far away. I needed a medium-sized city where I could get a good job and take care of my children."

"Doesn't your husband help?"

"Yes, he's fairly generous with child support and has promised to take care of their education. My attorney said I did not ask for enough child support, but I didn't want to ask for any more than I felt I really needed to make it."

"When is your divorce final?"

"I just filed last week. It takes nine months.

"Well, that will pass quickly," he said and squeezed her hand.

Rory stopped at a small town which, he said, had erupted with the discovery of gold, accommodated tens of thousands of miners, shopkeepers, and opportunists until the gold ran out. Now it was a quiet, quaint village filled with tourists in summer and almost deserted in winter. They parked in a lot covered with odd yellow-colored dirt, its surface broken now and then by a few anemic-looking weeds and tufts of grass.

"It's probably waste from a mine," Rory said, as Amanda knelt to take a closer look. "It may have been a hundred feet underground at one time."

They walked on narrow, cracked, and uneven sidewalks, admiring the turn-of-the-century buildings. Shops displayed rocks, pieces of mining machinery, and yellowing photographs of men wearing derby hats and women in long dark dresses trimmed with wide lace. Donkeys stood here and there in the street, harnessed to tiny colorful wagons, waiting patiently alongside their lounging owners for fares. A stately hotel filled most of a block. An elegant card with scalloped edges, affixed to a window next to the lobby entrance, proclaimed that rooms, furnished in the original style, with modernized baths, were available at reasonable prices. Good food, and nightly melodramas were additional attractions. Amanda and Rory peeked into the lobby, which looked like the set for a western movie, and they decided that they must return one day for an overnight stay.

They snacked on ice cream cones in an outdoor courtyard and watched the sun slide behind the mountain peaks.

"What is the altitude here?" Amanda asked as she slipped her arms into her cardigan, when a chilly breeze wafted down the slopes.

"About 8,000 feet, I think. It gets cool when the sun goes down."

They walked to the car and began driving back. Suddenly Rory reached under the seat of the car and pulled out a harmonica. He began to play a popular song, then another and another, stopping at intervals to sing some of the lyrics.

Amanda was entranced. No one had ever sung to her before. She laid her head back against the seat and closed her eyes, enjoying this novelty and Rory's strong tenor voice.

As they started down the pass, Rory put the harmonica away. He reached for Amanda's hand and held it in his lap. She smiled contentedly, and nestled further into the seat.

"Amanda, what shall we plan for this week? We can do something different every day."

"Rory! Don't you think we should—well, cool it a bit? Besides, I'm not finished unpacking, and...."

"Okay," he said and laughed, "we'll talk about it later. But how about the weekend?"

"I plan to drive to my parents' early Saturday to see my kids."

"How long a drive is it? When will you be back?"

"About five hours, I think. I'll be back late Sunday night."

"Um." He turned the radio to a music station and sang along off and on.

In the city, he made several turns and stopped at the edge of a small park. Amanda looked at him, puzzled. She remembered the sudden stop in the parking lot the other night. She wondered what this was all about. Rory stopped the engine, turned and took her hands in his.

"Amanda, I've only known you a couple of weeks. When we met, I thought we might be friends—have dinner, maybe go dancing, and have some fun. I've not dated much since my divorce, and I wasn't looking for anyone special." He paused, gazed out the window at the darkness and took a deep breath as he turned back toward her. "I don't understand this … but I think about you all the time. I wonder what you are doing, and I want to be there—wherever you are."

His face was inches from hers. She could see a small frown on his forehead, and his eyes seemed very dark.

"I don't understand, either, Rory." she whispered. "I like being with you, too—it's really crazy, almost eerie."

"Maybe it is crazy. It doesn't make much sense. I never believed in … but I know one thing. I know I love you, Amanda, I love you." His grip on her hands tightened, becoming almost painful.

Amanda sat in stunned silence. "I love you, Amanda, I love you," the words swirled over and over in her mind. She resisted the impulse to yawn or cough, thinking the altitude had affected her hearing. Surely she had misunderstood. She sat statue-like, staring at his face in the darkness. Her mind willed her mouth to open and words to come forth, but it would not obey. The silence became oppressive. Suddenly, Rory pulled her into his arms. He kissed her nose, her eyelids, her mouth. Amanda responded, her senses heightened. She could feel Rory's heart beating as he pulled her closer. After a few moments he released her, emitting a soft, strange laugh—a mixed sound of unbelief, uncertainty, and bafflement. The same utterance, yet softer, escaped from Amanda, as she fell back in the seat. Rory started the car and drove to Amanda's house, whistling a melody Amanda did not recognize.

Outside her door, Rory kissed her tenderly. “I meant what I said. I love you.” He brushed her face with his fingers. “I'll call you tomorrow. Good night.” And he was gone.

5

And be renewed in the spirit of your mind

(Ephesians 4:23)

Amanda dropped into a chair and tried to sort out her feelings and her thoughts. It was too great a task. She forced her mind into neutral and prepared for bed. "I'll think about this tomorrow," she said aloud and then giggled, thinking of Scarlet saying similar words. Her dreams were disturbing and she woke with a headache. She had overslept and had to rush.

She had lunch at her desk and called Debbie.

"Amanda, how are you? I've called you several times in the last few days," said Debbie, after Amanda identified herself.

"I'm fine. I'd like to talk to you. Is it all right if I come over after work?"

"Sure, I'll be home. Is anything wrong?"

"No … that is, I don't know. I don't think so."

"Amanda?"

"I'll see you this afternoon."

Amanda struggled to concentrate as the afternoon dragged.

Finally, a few minutes after five, she pulled into Debbie's drive. Sarah and Anne ran to her as she got out of the car and she stooped to pick each up in turn for a whirling hug. Debbie waved from the patio where flames were rising from the charcoal grill.

"Come and have some iced tea. You'll stay for supper? We're having grilled chicken."

"Hi, Deb!" Amanda sat on a bench, stretching her legs out in front of her and drank thirstily from the glass Debbie offered her; a little girl sat on either side of her.

"Rough day? You look beat," commented Debbie.

"Aunt Amanda, we saw a squirrel at the park," Sarah said, tugging at Amanda's sleeve.

"Sarah spilled her milk on Mommy's clean floor this morning and Mommy said...." Anne was not to be outdone in giving Amanda the latest news.

Debbie interrupted. "Girls, go swing for awhile. You can tell Aunt Amanda later."

Amanda smiled and waved as the girls reluctantly obeyed. She watched as they began to swing higher and higher. Their laughter split the afternoon quiet. Max, the family German shepherd, lay on the grass keeping watch, occasionally raising his head to bark, as though warning the girls to be careful. A slight breeze stirred the leaves of the honey locust tree, cooling the air. She lifted her face to the westering sun and breathed deeply.

"It's very peaceful here, Debbie."

"Peaceful! With all that noise?" Debbie rolled her eyes and laughed.

Amanda laughed with her. "It's all perspective. I miss my kids—their laughter, hugs, and kisses, even their bickering, and, yes, even their noise. They're having a great time, Mama says. They haven't asked many questions about all this. At first, I was glad about that, but ... Mama says they haven't talked about leaving their home and friends or mentioned their dad. Anyway, I'm going down this weekend. Would you and David like to go with me?"

"We'd like to but David's company is having their annual picnic. I was going to invite you to go with us," said Debbie.

"Oh. Well, I may leave Friday after work. I'll be late getting there, but I will have more time to visit." Amanda sat silently, staring into the distance, unseeing.

"Is there something else you want to talk about? What have you been doing the last few days? Amanda?"

"What? Sorry, I was wool-gathering, I guess—all this mountain air."

"Okay. Work is fine, kids are fine; problems with the house?"

"No, no, nothing like that. I…." Amanda laughed nervously. "I've been seeing the man who fixed my refrigerator."

"I see. Rory, is it?"

"Rory, yes. We've gone out several times, and … Debbie, it's weird, uncanny—we have so much in common." She stopped, wondering if that was really true. "At any rate, he's easy to be with, no awkwardness at all. We talk about all sorts of things, and he's so …" she groped for the right word, gave up and settled for "nice. Sounds trite and rather boring and that's not it, but, in the best sense of the word, he's really nice." She looked at Debbie, imploring understanding.

Debbie grinned. "You really hit it off, huh? Great! That's wonderful! It's about time you had some fun. So what's the problem?"

"I'm scared. Everything is going too fast. Mostly, I don't ever want to be hurt again." She paused and took a deep breath. "Last night Rory said he loved me, and … and I almost said I loved him, too. It's insane. We've just met and I don't *want* to love anyone right now." She burst into tears.

Debbie sat down on the bench and put her arms around Amanda.

"I don't know what to do. I tried to pray about it last night, but I fell asleep without an answer," Amanda said.

"Did you burn yourself, Aunt Amanda?" Amanda raised her head and looked into Anne's anxious eyes.

She hastily wiped her eyes. "No, sweetheart. I'm fine. Aren't grownups silly sometimes?" She smiled and tickled Anne. "Oh, I almost forgot!" She rummaged in her handbag. "Here—one for you, and one for you, Sarah," who was standing behind Anne with her thumb in her mouth. Amanda handed each child a tiny gold nugget on a thin gold chain.

"It's pretty, but what is it?" asked Anne.

"A piece of gold—from the pot at the end of the rainbow," teased Amanda. "Let me help you put it on."

"Mommy, look!" said Sarah. "Put it on me, please."

Debbie hooked the chain around Sarah's neck and stood admiring them. "There, you both look beautiful. Now go watch for Daddy so you can show him." She patted both little bottoms and the girls ran toward the drive.

"Stay for supper, Amanda. We can talk more after the girls are in bed."

"All right, I'd like that. What can I do to help?"

David arrived and admired the girls' necklaces. They sat at the outside table enjoying the chicken and salad. Later, Amanda helped bathe the girls and tuck them into their beds. David read them a story while Amanda and Debbie did the dishes. Then the three of them settled at the kitchen table with steaming mugs of fresh coffee.

"So, Amanda, job going okay? And how is the car doing?"

"The job is okay, not difficult, and the car runs fine," answered Amanda.

Silence. David looked from Debbie to Amanda and back to Debbie. They both appeared to be miles away.

"Debbie, what's going on?" he asked. "Amanda?"

Slowly, Amanda repeated most of what she had confided to Debbie earlier. David listened without interrupting.

"I'm going to check this guy out," he said when she had finished. "I know some people who probably know him."

"David, you can't do that!" Amanda sputtered.

"Sure I can. I want to know what kind of person he is."

Debbie broke in, "Amanda, bring him to supper tomorrow night. Then you can see for yourself, David."

"Good idea, but I'll still ask around," promised David.

"Amanda, will you bring him? I know it's short notice."

"I guess … yes, I would like both of you to meet him. We'll come if he's free," decided Amanda. "I must get home. Rory is supposed to call about eight. Thanks, I love you two." She gave them hugs and thanked Debbie for the supper and left.

6

He is my refuge and my fortress

(Psalm 91:2)

The phone was ringing as Amanda unlocked her door. She ran to pick up the receiver. "Hello."

"Hi, are you all right? I've been calling," Rory's concerned voice came over the line.

"I had supper with my brother and sister-in-law," she explained, and glanced at her watch. "It's not quite eight."

"Yes, well, the Jaycees meeting wasn't very interesting or important, so I left early. May I come over?"

"All right. I have something to ask you. You can't stay long, though. I must wash my hair."

"Be there in fifteen minutes," and the phone went dead.

Amanda put her things away, combed her hair and made coffee. She heard the car door slam as she took mugs from the cupboard, then a knock on the door. Rory smiled as she opened it and he handed her a single red rose.

Amanda inhaled the fragrance of the rose, and smiled her appreciation. She left to find a vase and Rory sat on the couch. "So how is your brother … David is it? … and Diane?"

"Debbie. David and Debbie." Amanda sat beside him. He took her hand, leaned his head back and put his feet on the coffee table.

"Ah. This feels good. This new job is different than any I've ever had. I'm tired."

"Do you like it?"

"Yes, I think so. It takes some getting used to."

"Want some coffee? I just made it."

"Love some." He squeezed her hand and released it as she rose and went toward the kitchen.

"My sister-in-law invited us to dinner tomorrow night," she called. "Would you like to go?"

"You mean me, too? She invited me?"

"Yes, silly, both of us. They want to meet you." She blushed, thinking of David's words. "Will you come?"

"I'd like to—if you want to?" He looked at her questioningly as she re-entered the room with a tray. She smiled and nodded her head, placed the tray on the table, and handed him a cup.

"Store bought cookies, I'm afraid, but they're pretty good," she said as she offered him the plate.

Rory ate two or three cookies, sipped some of the coffee, and leaned back with his eyes closed. Amanda sat in the corner of the couch with her legs folded under her. She watched him as she sipped her coffee, cradling the mug in her hands, and wondered if he had fallen asleep. His voice startled her.

"Are you still going to your parents place this weekend?"

"Yes, Friday, I think, right after work."

"I'd like to go with you."

Amanda choked, quickly set her cup down, and wiped her mouth. "You want to go to my parents'?" she asked.

"Why not? I want to meet them and your kids. Tell me their names and ages again. Is that a picture of them?" he asked pointing to the framed photograph on the end table.

Amanda picked up the photo, taken about a year ago, and handed it to Rory. She identified each child by name and age.

Rory studied the photo for a moment. "They're cute kids. Well, what do you say? Am I invited?"

"You're really serious, aren't you?"

"I'm serious, Honey." He slid off the couch, one knee on the floor, and took her hands in his. His eyes held hers. "We'll do this right!" he said, his eyes never wavering. "Amanda, I love you. I want to spend my life with you. Will you marry me?"

Amanda gasped. She studied his face and knew he was not teasing her. She could not draw her eyes away. Finally, she spoke. "Marriage! Rory, we've just met … I don't…." She stopped, she was flabbergasted and didn't know what to say.

As if he had read her thoughts, he said, "Don't say anything right now … think about it. I didn't mean to spring it on you like that. But I thought I had made it clear how I felt."

Amanda sat frozen, silent, her face pale, her eyes staring into his.

"Amanda?" Rory rose to his feet and bent over her. "Sweetheart?"

She took a deep breath, color returned to her cheeks and to her chagrin, tears formed in her eyes.

"Hey, it's not that bad, is it?" Rory shook her gently and grinned at her. "Are you all right?"

Amanda wiped at her eyes. "I'm sorry. You almost shocked the life out of me. I never expected…."

"It's okay. We'll talk about it later. Just sit there. I'll get more coffee." He picked up the cups and went to the kitchen.

He returned, handed Amanda her cup, and sat in the chair across from her.

Amanda took a sip of coffee. She tried to think. At last she raised her head. Rory was looking at her expectantly. Her heart beat faster and she felt giddy. She tried to organize her thoughts: *I do love him,*

I'm sure of that—and I don't believe I could stand it if he went away, but **marriage....** *I need to know there's absolute commitment to making it work, and we haven't talked about God enough, and....*

"Please give me a little time. I want to think. We need to talk, but I don't think I can right now." She smiled. "Do you understand? *Please* wait!" she pleaded.

"Sure, take all the time you need. I'll wait." His words were spoken cheerfully, but Amanda saw disappointment flash across his face, and his jaw was set with grim determination. Illogically, she sighed with relief at finding no hint of discouragement, as had it been there, it would have been of her own making.

Her eyes widened, not with surprise, but with a sudden awareness that this man would never let her down. They sat, not speaking, each caught in their private thoughts, for several minutes.

Then Rory rose from the chair and sat beside her on the couch. He leaned back, put his feet on the coffee table, and nonchalantly said, "Well, am I invited to your parents' or not?"

Amanda came back to earth. "Of course, if you really want to come. I'd like you to meet my children and my parents."

"Good," he said. "I'll pick you up about 5:30 Friday, and we can get sandwiches on the way."

"But we can take *my* car, not yours."

"We'll take mine. It needs a good run. All this city driving is hard on it."

She prudently gave way, gracefully. "Okay, but I'll pay for the gas."

"Why?" he asked.

"Why?" she echoed stupidly, "because ... I should ... I don't want ..." she floundered.

"Amanda," Rory said sternly, "You are not obligated to me for anything, and I'm not trying to press you into anything." His face softened. "I'll take care of the gas because I want to. Understand?"

"I didn't think—you really are wonderful, and special. I've never known anyone like you. Most … well, never mind. We'll do it your way." She smiled. "I would like to start back early afternoon on Sunday." Her smile disappeared. "Is *that* all right with you?"

Rory's eyes widened, and then he grinned widely. "Whenever you like, just tell me when you want to leave."

She checked her watch. "It's too late to let Mother know she has a houseguest for the weekend. I'll call her in the morning."

Rory rose and pulled her to her feet. "I'd better go. You kept me up too late and I need my beauty sleep," he teased. He brushed his fingers across her cheek and mouth. "You are so sweet. I don't know how I got so lucky." He kissed her gently, whispered "I love you," and was gone.

Amanda stood staring at the door for some minutes, then she turned and fell on her knees with her head in the chair.

"Abba Father, Lord Jesus, is this real? I *know* it isn't a ruse of any kind on Rory's part, but—Lord, did You bring him into my life? It's strange—my refrigerator being broken when it was almost new, the first man couldn't fix it, Rory coming on a Saturday when I was here, and on his last day of work. And, normally, he would not have asked me out—he said he wouldn't have dared. He risked getting fired, but since he was quitting any way.… How did all that happen! And we seem so right for each other. It isn't just coincidence, is it? I think I love him—I'm sure I do, but I don't want to make another mistake. Please let me make the right decision. Amen."

Hours later, she awoke with a start. Her legs were cramped and she was chilled. She glanced at her watch: 2:15! Slowly, she got to her feet and turned out the lights. As she brushed her teeth, she studied her reflection in the mirror—hair sticking every which way, pink splotches on her cheeks. "I look like a character in a horror movie." She giggled hysterically and climbed into bed.

Peace filled her heart and mind the next morning, and a joy she did not fully understand. A melody kept running through her mind—one that Rory had played on his harmonica. "This Song's For You," or something like that. The day passed quickly, though it was an effort to concentrate on her duties. Rory's words and the song kept going through her mind.

When she reached home that afternoon, she decided she had time for a quick shower before Rory arrived to go to Debbie and David's. She dressed with more care than usual, choosing a printed cotton, buttoned down the front with a wide white collar and simple white pumps. Her dark hair fell just to her shoulders in soft curls. She used little make-up—a little eye shadow, mascara, and lipstick. Her eyes were shiny and clear, her cheeks rosy. She had forgotten to call her mother that morning, and made a mental note to call without fail the next day.

Rory greeted her with a smile. "You look very pretty, tonight," he said as he put her in the car.

"Big brother wants to check me out, is that it?" Rory asked as they drove away, his eyes twinkling.

Amanda flushed. *If he only knew!* But she replied lightly, "Actually, he's my little brother—in age, not size!"

Amanda introduced Rory and David took him into the living room, while Amanda helped Debbie in the kitchen.

"He's nice looking, Amanda," commented Debbie, "and the way he looks at you!" She raised her eyebrows and giggled.

"Debbie," sighed Amanda, sinking into a chair at the table, "last night he asked me to marry him!"

"What? You're kidding!" Debbie stared at Amanda. "You're not kidding! What did you say?"

"I didn't say anything; I couldn't say anything. I was so shocked," admitted Amanda. "He wants to go with me this weekend—wants to meet the kids and Mama and Daddy."

Laughter drifted in from the living room. "They seem to be hitting it off," commented Debbie.

"They're alike in some ways," said Amanda, "that sort of weird sense of humor, you know? David isn't really going to 'check him out' is he?"

"I think he's already started. He said something about getting a line on him."

Anne and Sarah came into the kitchen. Debbie had fed them earlier and she now took them to a friend next door for the evening. Amanda finished setting the table, and they dished up the food when Debbie returned.

Dinner was excellent, though Debbie insisted she wasn't much of a cook. They ate the fried chicken, potatoes and gravy, and salad with enthusiasm, and finished with apple pie. The men kept Debbie and Amanda laughing with their jokes, as though they had a contest going. After clearing the table, they played hearts for a few hours, interrupted frequently by jokes.

Just before midnight, Amanda said they must leave or she would never make it to work in the morning. They put the cards away, not bothering to determine the winner.

David took Amanda aside. "Come into the girls' room. I want to show you the chest I'm making for them."

In the room, David asked Amanda to sit on the bed. "Amanda, I talked to a man who knows Rory. He says he's rather wild and has a quick temper. He belongs to the Jaycees and they sometimes have parties that get out of hand."

"David! I don't believe it. He's never shown any of those characteristics to me. Are you sure they were talking about Rory? I know he belongs to the Jaycees, but…."

"I just thought you should know. I admit, I didn't see anything like that tonight. We got along fine, and none of the jokes, even when we were alone, were off-color. He obviously thinks a lot of you, and I like the guy. Just be careful. I care what happens to you, you know." He took her by the shoulders and kissed her cheek.

"Here's the chest I'm making, but you can look at it another time."

Amanda rubbed her hand across the top of the smoothly sanded wood. "It's lovely David. You make such beautiful things."

"Thanks. Well, we had better get back to the others."

In the car, Amanda was preoccupied by David's information, and Rory was puzzled.

"Did I goof up tonight? I had a good time and I really like David and Debbie. Did I do something wrong?"

"No! It was a great evening, and I'm glad you had a good time. I'm a little tired, that's all, it's very late."

"I won't come in." Rory said as he handed her out of the car. "You get some sleep and I'll call you tomorrow." He kissed her lightly and left her at the door

7

In thee do I put my trust

(Psalm 7:1)

Amanda slowly walked down the hall to her bedroom. "What now, Father? I'm more confused than ever. This is like being on a roller coaster and I'm too exhausted to sort it out tonight. I'm trusting You, Father, to guide me. Please let it work out, for me, and for the children. I know they need a father, especially the boys. And I know You love them even more than I do. I put my life in Your hands, Father, as I have done many times. I've made a lot of mistakes and I don't always listen to Your Holy Spirit, and obey. But thank You for loving me, even when I mess up...." Her prayer tapered off and she fell asleep.

She awoke refreshed, with the sunlight peeking into her bedroom window. At seven, she called her mother. Catherine's bright, cheery voice warmed Amanda, as always. She apologized for not calling earlier, telling her about having dinner at David's and it being late when she got home.

"I'm coming Friday night. It will be late when I get there."

"That's fine, honey. The kids are anxious to see you.… No, they're fine. They just miss you. They're still sleeping."

"Don't wake them. Just give them kisses for me." She paused. "Mama? I'm bringing someone with me—a man I've been seeing. He wants to meet you and Daddy, and the kids. Is it all right?"

There was a short silence. "Well … of course.… I didn't know …?"

Amanda heard the question in her mother's voice. "I know, Mama, I hadn't said anything. I'll tell you all about it this weekend. I have to go to work now. I love you. And tell the kids I love them. Give Daddy a big hug. See you Friday."

She didn't want to discuss anything on the phone and hoped her mother wouldn't feel she was evading questions, which, of course, she was, she thought ruefully.

8

Hold up my goings in thy paths, that my footsteps slip not

(Psalm 17:5)

Rory called at six and said he had to work late. He would drop by if he finished before nine. Amanda tossed a few items she would need into the washing machine, then began to pack a small bag. She glanced at her watch at 9:30 and decided to make a cup of tea to take with her while she soaked in the tub. She would get to bed a little early. She had just slipped into her robe and reached for her hair curlers when she heard the knock on the door. Her watch said 10:12.

Oh, no! she thought as she hastily wrapped a towel around her head and hurried down the hall. At the door she paused, "Who is it?"

"Who were you expecting?" came Rory's voice through the door.

She opened the door a few inches. "I wasn't expecting anyone this late. I was just …" she touched the towel which swathed her head.

"You look beautiful. Could I get a cup of coffee? It's been a long day." He smiled at her. "I know it's late, but…"

"Well, just a few minutes, okay? No coffee's made. Instant okay, or hot tea?"

Rory grimaced. “No hot tea. How about ice water?”

Amanda laughed. “Come on in. I’ll get your water.”

Rory lounged on the couch as usual, with his feet on the coffee table and his eyes closed. Amanda placed the water glass beside his feet.

“You haven’t told me much about your new job. How is it going?” she asked, as she sat in the chair across from him.

“It’s pretty interesting—checking up on stolen credit cards and so forth. Tonight we had to pick up a car that the bank repossessed.”

“Rory! Is this job dangerous?”

“Not really. At least most of the time it’s routine. You run into some strange people sometimes, though.” He opened his eyes and looked at her. “I like your new hair-do. What do you call that?”

She grinned. “This is the latest style from Bali,” She stood and placed one hand on her hip, the other on her towel-turban, bent one leg at the knee and balanced on her bare toes. “You’re seeing me at my worst. I shouldn’t have let you in.” She plopped on the couch beside him.

He sat up. “If this is your worst....” He nuzzled her ear. “Hmm, you smell good enough to eat.”

He held her face in his hands and kissed her nose, her eyes, and finally her mouth, then pulled her close with her head against his chest. He held her for a long moment, then whispered in her ear.

“You are so sweet, so little, so soft.”

He turned her face to his and kissed her again, and she eagerly responded. Finally, she pulled away, breathless.

“You had better go,” she said quietly.

His eyes were dark blue, almost black in the shadow of the lamplight behind him, and she sat, caught in his gaze.

Abruptly, he stood, pulling her up with him. “Yes, I’d better go, sweetheart. I’ll call or come by tomorrow.” His lips brushed hers lightly. “Remember, I love you.”

Amanda took a deep breath and whispered, “I love you, too.”

He squeezed her to him, quickly released her, and went out the door.

Amanda picked up the towel that had fallen to the floor. She rolled her hair in curlers and climbed into bed, barely aware of what she was doing. Her last thoughts before sleep overcame her were *This is real! Rory is real!* "Thank You, Father, for this man. I am trusting You that he is right for me."

The next day went quickly, though she tended to daydream at times. Her boss was polite and cool when speaking to her, and was out of the office most of the day, for which she was very grateful. On the way home, she pondered what small gifts she could take to the kids, her sisters, and her parents. The phone was ringing as she unlocked her door just before six. It was Debbie.

"Amanda, David asked me to call you. He wanted me to tell you that Rory's wild times were apparently right after his wife left. I guess he took it pretty hard. Apparently she was running around with Rory's best friend and she just took the baby and left (I think the guy left with her). He found a note when he got home."

"Thanks, Debbie. Rory has told me a little about what happened. I guess I can understand that as well as anyone, although I handled it a bit differently. People act strangely when they've been hurt. Sometimes you just don't care anymore. I had the children to help keep me on an even keel. He had no one."

"You're probably right. I'm sure everything is okay now. Are you still going home this weekend? And is Rory going with you?"

"Yes, and yes," laughed Amanda. "We're leaving Friday after work. I called Mama. It surprised her I think."

"Well, give them our love and have a safe trip. Rory has the surprise—meeting your large family. I remember it well!"

Amanda laughed. "Yes, I know, I've tried to prepare him for it. He has only one sister. By the way, Rory enjoyed the other night; said he hoped you would invite him again. I think he enjoys family things. I have to go, Debbie. I'll call you when I get back."

At the shopping center, Amanda bought chocolates for her parents, nail polish for her sisters, a new softball for the boys and a doll outfit for Elizabeth's doll. Back home, she finished packing and opened a can of soup for her supper. She was rinsing the few dishes when Rory arrived. When she opened the door, he handed her a small bouquet of wild flowers.

"I was in the foothills this afternoon. These were everywhere beside the road and I thought you might like them."

"They're lovely," said Amanda as she smelled their fragrance. "What a sweet thing to do. I love flowers. Thank you for being so thoughtful."

"I plan to do lots of things to make you smile like that," Rory told her.

"Would you like some soup? Vegetable beef … only take a moment to heat," Amanda asked.

"Soup sounds good. I planned to get here earlier and we could go out for something, but I got held up."

Amanda heated soup and made a small garden salad. Rory found a bowl and spoon, and caught her in a brief hug every time he passed by her.

"The soup will scorch, you silly," protested Amanda.

Rory grinned as he caught her again, "This is more fun than eating soup!"

Eventually, he sat eating while Amanda gnawed on a carrot.

"Tell me again about your family. Who will be there?" Rory said between bites.

Amanda went to her bedroom and returned with a photo album. "This is Mama and Daddy. These are my youngest sisters: Sue and Jeanette. Jeanette is actually younger than Matthew and Joshua. I hardly know her or Sue because I've lived away so many years. I have two other sisters and another brother who are married.

I'm not sure you'll meet them, but my sister Kate and my brother Ed live nearby...."

"It's a big family. As I've said, I have one sister. My parents are divorced. My grandmother died last year. She and Grandad lived next door when I was growing up. He taught me a lot. And Andrew … here's a picture of him when he was two. I don't know where he is—somewhere with his mother and her new husband."

"He's so cute! He looks like you. You haven't seen him since...."

"Since she left—about three years ago."

"I'm so sorry, Rory."

"Yeah, well … changing the subject, I was filling out forms for insurance at work. Do you think it's important to have barrel insurance? Grandad has it, I know, he told me when Grandmother died, but I don't really think I need it. Do you carry barrel insurance?"

Amanda searched her brain, his Texas accent sometimes baffled her. "Barrel insurance? I don't think I … what is barrel insurance?" she asked.

Rory gave her a strange look. "Barrel insurance—for your barrel."

Enlightenment came and Amanda burst into laughter. Tears streamed down her face. Rory stared at her in amazement. Finally she could speak.

"You're saying *burial* insurance?" She managed to squeak out the words before again succumbing to laughter.

Rory was perplexed. "That *is* what I said, burial insurance."

"I thought you … said … b-a-r-r-e-l insurance.... I couldn't figure out what kind of … barrels you would have to insure!" Unbidden, laughter bubbled up inside her again. She fought for control.

"Rory, I'm so sorry, but—it's just too funny!" And off she went again.

"You thought …!" Rory joined in the laughter.

Finally, Amanda wiped her eyes with her napkin. "I haven't laughed so much in ages. I hope you aren't angry?"

"You're cute when you laugh. I like to watch you. I just didn't realize I was so amusing."

"I love your accent, Rory," Amanda was ashamed of herself. "You must think I speak differently, too, sometimes. I have no idea what kind of accent I have. I'm half English and half Italian, but we didn't speak Italian at home, and Mama doesn't have an accent. She didn't learn Italian either."

Rory took her hand. "Whatever it is, I like it," he said. "I have to leave, though I don't want to. Have to wash out some socks and things. Jeans and sport shirt all right for this trip?"

"Oh, sure. Just casual," said Amanda.

She walked with him to the door, returned his kiss with pleasure, and he was gone.

Amanda took a deep breath. She sat in a chair, thinking. *This guy really gets to me. He's fun, he brings me flowers, he makes me feel wonderful. I feel important—that I'm worth something. I have confidence in working. I know I'm a good secretary, and I think I'm a good mother. It's a thrill to watch the kids grow and expand their world. But as a woman, I've had no confidence for a long time. I've felt like a zero. Rory has changed that. I feel totally alive for the first time in years.* She smiled, remembering the past hour. *There was a different side of Rory tonight, one I hadn't seen before. He always seems so in charge, in control, but tonight, there was a little-boy quality mixed in—a little vulnerability and naivete which is very appealing.* She sighed, happily. *It's great to feel cared for, for a change. I love how I feel—like Phoenix rising from the ashes.* She giggled self-consciously at her fanciful thoughts, then her face became thoughtful, serious. *I love this man's personality. He's real—no masks, no pretenses, no guile. I trust him. I will trust him with my heart.* A fragment of a poem came floating into her thoughts: "Across the … of my heart, I wrote 'No thoroughfare,' But love … cried, 'I enter everywhere!'"[2] "Oh Jesus, thank You! Thank You for this blessing!"

She rose abruptly and went to her bedroom. She finished preparations and slept, soundly, until the alarm woke her. Work was uneventful and the hours went slowly. At last it was five o'clock, and she could leave.

Rory arrived soon after she got home and they were on their way. They stopped for hamburgers and soon left the city traffic behind. Rory retrieved his harmonica from under the seat. Amanda relaxed, letting the sound wrap her in contentment. Many tunes—some familiar classical, some she couldn't name; "Shenandoah," one of her favorites, and then, "This Song's For You." Rory laid the harmonica aside, took Amanda's hand and began to sing softly in his clear, tenor voice, "This Song's For You." He squeezed her hand.

"I can hardly wait to start giving you things. Everything to make you happy—to put that sparkle in your eyes."

Amanda smiled and held his hand tightly. "There's not really very much I want," she said, "just someone I can trust."

He looked at her gravely, "You can trust me. I promise you that."

Amanda's thoughts went over the time they had spent together. She had thought at first that Rory was about her age, perhaps a little younger. But several things had come up that made her wonder. She had ignored them, perhaps because she was afraid of the truth. Now she realized she had to know and she was angry with herself for not finding out sooner. Abruptly, she asked, "How old are you?"

"What difference does that make?" he asked, puzzled. "I'm almost twenty-five."

Amanda gasped. "No, that can't be right! You're teasing me! You can't be serious!" She wanted to scream. She couldn't breathe. *Father, how could You let this happen? It's cruel, it's too much. No, I* ***won't*** *believe it!* She became aware of Rory speaking.

"... but I don't know what it has to do with anything. I like women who are...."

Her head whirled and she tuned out his voice. Nine years, nine!

She had thought, perhaps four—at the most, but … it was too much. It would never work. She felt crushed, betrayed somehow. Tears blurred her vision, and she felt faint. This is more than I can take, *why* didn't I ask earlier? I could have prevented this! Tears streamed down her face.

Amanda was unaware that Rory had slowed and soon found a safe place to pull off the freeway. His voice broke through her misery.

"Amanda! Amanda! Look at me!" The command in his voice startled her and she lifted her eyes to his dark green ones. The anger lurking there sobered her. He was angry with her!

"Amanda," his gaze held her motionless, "I love you, do you hear me? I love you, and I think you love me. Age has nothing to do with it. It's *ridiculous* to even consider it, to even have this conversation."

"No," she whispered, "It isn't ridiculous. It's impossible. The gap is too much. It's wrong. It can't be." She dropped her head into her hands, and sobbed hopelessly. "I can't believe this is happening to me. It's all my fault. I should have asked. I'm sorry; I'm so sorry. Please, take me back home. I can't go on. I want to go home!"

"No! I'm not taking you home. You listen to me!" He grasped her arms and shook her.

"Please, let me go. Please take me back. I can't take any more!"

Rory shook her again. "Listen to me!" He cupped her face in his hand and forced her to face him. "You're going to make me mad in a minute. Don't you think I knew about how old you are? The ages of your kids? I knew. If it had been a problem, I would have handled it then."

Amanda blinked back tears, struggling to comprehend his words. Of course, he would have known, because of the kids. And he never said anything—anything at all.

"It doesn't matter! Do you hear me? Do you understand? I don't care: it's *you* I want."

Amanda tried to grasp what he was saying. "But in twenty

years—thirty years? What about then? You'll feel...." She stopped; tears streamed down her cheeks, spilling into her lap.

"What? What will I feel? Do you know my feelings now? Do you think I'm making them up, or just imagining them? Is that what love means to you? Here today, gone tomorrow! Is that what you think it means to me? That's pretty insulting, Amanda!"

Amanda gasped, her eyes widened in shock. "I didn't mean...."

"You don't give me much credit, do you? Look, Amanda, I know you've been hurt, but I'm not like that man. I know what I want, and I know how I feel. What I feel is real and it's permanent. You'll have to trust me. I can't prove it to you today, but I will prove it in all the days to come. I want to make you happy—always. I want to take care of you and your children."

He wiped her face with his handkerchief. "I don't like these tears. As soon as your divorce is final, we'll get married. I'll show you what real love is. Do you understand me, Amanda?"

She nodded her head, reluctantly. Although she was not totally convinced, Rory's words were penetrating her fears and they were dissolving. He kissed her tenderly.

"I do love you, Rory. I don't know how it happened—I didn't want to ... I've been so scared!" She closed her eyes and clenched her trembling hands. "I didn't mean to hurt you. I want to trust you. I want to believe you. It's not your fault that I have this problem. I failed once, and I don't know what I did wrong." Again tears coursed down her face.

"This is the last time we will discuss this. I don't know all the circumstances, but I know you. It's not your fault. You're everything a man could want. I will never hurt you, Amanda, I promise. I may make some mistakes, but I will never deliberately hurt you. Will you believe me?"

Again she nodded, this time with more conviction.

Rory took her into his arms. His voice shook with emotion. "I love you so much. I'll never let you get away." He held her for a long time. She clung to him and slowly her anxiety and fears began to dissipate. She felt drained. Then peace slipped in, filling her emptiness.

Rory released her. He looked at her white, tear-ravaged face. She looked into his eyes, now a warm clear blue.

"I want to see a smile," he told her, and when she managed a weak one, he turned to start the car, and glanced down at his clothes.

"Look what you did to my shirt? What will your mother say?" he teased.

Amanda glanced at the damp spots covering most of his shirt front, and gave him a watery smile. "She'll think you don't know how to iron."

"You don't realize how pretty you are when you smile," he said, as he started the car and carefully drove back onto the freeway. He began to sing "This Song's For You."

9

I will sing praise to thy name

(Psalm 9:2)

Amanda sat very close to him, her left hand resting on his knee. Her heart sang along with Rory's voice, although she was exhausted. After some time, they began to discuss their future, squeezing each other's hand every few moments and reveling in their joy. After a short silence, they both began to speak at once.

"You first," said Rory.

"I was just thinking about the last few weeks—all the odd things that have happened."

"That's what I was thinking—too many coincidences."

"Yes, or maybe, not coincidences. My fridge not working. . . ."

"And John couldn't fix it."

"So *you* had to come—on a Saturday when I was there."

"And, as I told you, if it hadn't been my last day, I would never have asked you out."

"I wasn't ready to see anyone. Later, I hoped, but not yet."

"I wasn't planning on a relationship, either. My life was all right—sort of carefree, you know."

Amanda's voice became more serious. "Rory, we haven't talked about God very much. You told me you were a Christian, but …" she paused to gather courage, "have you been baptized?"

"Twice!" Rory exclaimed. "Once when I was a kid. A year ago or so, a minister told me it didn't take the first time, so he baptized me again!"

"You're not serious?" Amanda laughed. "Did it take that time?"

"It took. I believe Jesus died for my sins, rose again, and sits in heaven beside God the Father." They looked at each other in the dim light from the dash. "Okay?" he asked.

A big smile lit her face. "Very okay. I believe that, too, and I believe Jesus is my Friend, and that He cares about what is happening—to us, I mean. I believe He arranges things."

"You mean … you think … Whew, that's heavy." He became thoughtful and Amanda waited quietly.

"I guess it would explain what has happened, but do you really think He bothers about that sort of thing? Big problems I can understand—how wars come out, saving someone's life—I believe that, but would He do this for us?"

"I think He did. I know He answers prayer and sometimes not the way you think He will, but His way is always better. He's been very close, or perhaps I should say I've been very close to Him the last few months. I've prayed and prayed. Mostly, what I do is just talk to Jesus—like a friend, and He has helped me get through the mess I was in. I don't know what I would have done without Him."

"And you think He arranged for us to meet, and all the rest of this?"

"I think He may have. Of course, we're not forced to do anything about it if we don't want to, but He gave us the opportunity."

They smiled at each other, and then began to laugh. It went on and on. Joy streamed from them until they were breathless. Then silence filled the car as each contemplated what had taken place.

After a while Rory spoke, "I will thank God every day for giving you to me."

Amanda's eyes were shining. "Me, too.

Later, Amanda pointed out landmarks and mentioned the many coal mines scattered throughout the area. Her grandfather had worked there one winter long ago, when times were hard, leaving her grandmother and the children alone on their farm until the spring. She remembered Raton Pass before the freeway went through—a narrow, winding two-lane road.

"Every few miles a steep incline would veer off to the right," she told him, "and trucks heavily loaded with coal would sometimes lose their brakes or the truck could not be downshifted to a lower gear. Then the driver would steer the truck up the incline to slow it and if he could not get it stopped, he would jump out before the truck reached the end of the incline and plummeted into a canyon."

They turned east as the last of the sun's rays peaked over the mountain range. There was Sierra Grande, a huge peak in front and slightly to their right. She told him of a terrible fire there when she was a child. It had spread far up the sides of the mountain and surrounded the base, even jumping the highway in several places. Men from miles around had fought the blaze for several days.

"That is Capulin Mountain," she said, pointing to the north. "It's an extinct volcano."

"Really!" Rory peered through the side window. "It looks like there is a road winding around it. Can you drive up there?"

"Yes. I've been up several times. We can do that one day when we have more time."

"You can see down inside?"

"Yes, you can walk down into it."

Dusk was settling in the valleys. Small herds of white-faced cattle could be seen here and there in the grassy pastures that reached to the foothills on the north and the horizon on the south. Gradually, they gave way to cultivated fields of golden wheat, stripped of their brilliance in the growing darkness, and arrow-straight furrows with tiny green plants peeping over.

It was good to be going home, Amanda thought, and she greeted each old landmark as it appeared on the landscape. They were very near the end of their journey.

"Oh, there's the new bridge! Mama said they had finished it," Amanda said as the car moved on to a modern concrete spillway type of bridge.

"What happened to the old one?" asked Rory, as the headlights picked up its remains several yards downstream. Sand filled the streambed, except for a trickle of water, perhaps two feet wide in the center.

"It was washed away in a flood," said Amanda.

"But there's no water!"

Amanda laughed. "You're right. It's more like an arroyo than a river–almost dry, except when there are heavy rains up in the mountains. Then the water comes rushing down and sometimes runs over the banks."

Rory grinned. "I'll have to see that to believe it!"

In a few minutes, they arrived at the farm. It was very late, but the children had been allowed to stay up. Amanda hugged her children until they squealed for mercy. Finally, she released them and introduced Rory, who had been standing just inside the door. Amanda's father, James, took Rory to the living room. The children stared at him, puzzled and suspicious, but soon turned back to their mother. After a half hour or so, Amanda's mother suggested they get some sleep and explained the arrangements she had made. Amanda would have her old room, and Rory should be comfortable in the boys' (Amanda's two brothers) room. Joshua and Matthew would sleep on the couch-bed. Elizabeth clung to her mother, so Amanda told her she could stay with her and tucked her into her bed. She held her close while Elizabeth said her prayers and promptly fell asleep. Amanda began to pray. Her heart was so full of thanksgiving, she could not contain her joy in prayer-thoughts. She carefully slipped from the bed to the floor and her thoughts became soft whispers, praising her Father, her Redeemer and Friend, and the Holy Spirit, who had been so responsible for what was happening to her. After many minutes, she felt the peace that defies understanding, and returned to the bed. Her last thoughts were of Rory, wondering if he was thinking of her.

10

A time to heal

(Ecclesiastes 3:3)

Amanda woke early to muted voices downstairs. She smiled. No matter what time her parents went to bed, they were up at dawn the next morning. She heard the back door close and a soft whistle as her father called Butch, the family dog, to help with the morning chores. The sound of a pan clanging told her that her mother was starting breakfast. She stretched her legs luxuriously, savoring a few minutes before going down to help, and looked around the room that had been hers, and was now designated as the guest room. It looked much the same. A few of her knickknacks still graced the top of the wooden chest. The curtains and spread were new—light green and white instead of the purple she had insisted on when she was 14. Arrows of sunlight pierced the filmy curtains at the open window, shot unsteadily across the bed covers and halfway up the opposite wall. The sound of sparrows praising God for the daybreak floated in on sweet-smelling puffs of air.

She hugged the covers to her, thinking how happy she had been growing up here, and now, after a long absence, happiness was reaching out to her once more. She sighed with contentment and raised up on one elbow to gaze at her daughter sleeping beside her. Elizabeth, so precious. Her long lashes lay quietly on her cheeks, which were lightly sprinkled with freckles, hiding inquisitive blue eyes. Long brown hair, slightly reddish from the summer sun, was tightly confined in braids only one of which was visible, curling under her chin. Amanda swallowed the lump that rose in her throat, as she gazed at this priceless gift God had given her—and not just one, but three. She had been blessed. She gently touched Elizabeth's head with her fingers, then carefully got out of bed. She dressed quickly and silently, and stepped out into the hall, wondering if Rory was awake, in the room two doors down.

Downstairs, her mother was patting out biscuit dough. She greeted Amanda with a kiss on the cheek, mindful of her floury hands, and pointed to the rack of mugs hanging on the wall near the big Pyrex percolator, burping gently on the burner. Her father was at chores outdoors, and Matthew and Joshua were still asleep in the living room, Catherine told her. Amanda poured a cup of coffee and stood watching her mother.

"It's been a long time since I've watched you make breakfast," she said with a smile.

"It's good to have you home, Amanda. We've enjoyed the children, too. They're good kids."

Amanda turned her face away, fighting back tears, and changed the subject by asking about the farm, and Catherine complied. Wheat harvest was half over—good crop this year. God had blessed them. Fall crops would need rain soon. There were about thirty calves to be sold in the fall. Her father had bought a bigger combine. Amanda must gather fresh vegetables from the garden to take back with her, as well as some for David and Debbie. Amanda listed attentively. It had been a long time since she had given much thought to crops and calves. After another sip of coffee, she began to help with the meal preparation. They decided to let the children sleep yet awhile, but Amanda's father would want his breakfast as soon as he finished outdoors.

The sound of James scraping his feet on the outside mat sent them scurrying to dish up the food. He entered with a big smile for his eldest daughter and gave her his usual form of greeting his children—a strong pat on the back and a bear hug. His tall, straight figure towered over Amanda. Her head just reached the middle of his chest.

They sat eating and talking in low voices about how the children were adjusting, how Sue and Jeanette were enjoying teaching them about life on the farm, and Amanda's job, her house, and her car. Amanda knew the questions in her parents' minds were about Rory, but she wanted to speak privately with her mother first, so she chattered on. She told them she had decided it was best for the children to stay with them until the end of summer, if they still agreed? They did, with enthusiasm. She didn't know what to do about the time when they got home from school and she got off work—always a problem to find someone she could trust to care for them, and one she had faced several times in the past.

Then the others appeared, almost at the same time, clamoring for breakfast. The next hour was busy. James took Rory on a tour of the farm, the children ate, completed their chores, and went outside while Amanda and Catherine cleaned up the kitchen. It was almost time to prepare lunch when Amanda was able to draw her mother outside for a walk.

They visited the vegetable garden, with its rows and rows of plants in various shades of green—delicate lime-colored leaves of lettuce, dark green tomato plants, decorated with posies of yellow flowers and little green buttons holding the promise of juicy red fruit, rows of bright green, lifting white blossoms high, as well as drooping from the weight of clusters of long, narrow green beans, ("Need picking," Catherine commented), feathery carrot tops, squash with golden blossoms, cucumbers, okra, pumpkins, and more. A veritable super market! This bounty was bordered by multicolored zinnias, just coming into bloom, and spiky iris, their flowers spent, resting till the next spring.

"My, your garden is certainly thriving, Mama!"

"The children have helped. They don't particularly like weeding and hoeing, but they really enjoy harvesting," said Catherine, smiling. "They are good little workers—most of the time," she added, her eyes twinkling.

"It's so good for them to have chores where they can clearly see the results of their labor. I learned a lot about life working in this garden."

They left the garden and walked slowly down the lane. Amanda began to talk, sporadically, at first, then with more confidence. She started with the Saturday morning Rory came to check her refrigerator, and related all the events of the past few weeks, omitting the dramatic details of last evening, and ended with her misgivings over the difference in ages and yet how they believed the Lord had brought them together.

Catherine listened without interrupting until Amanda finished. Then she took her daughter into her arms.

"You know we only want you to be happy, dear. If you love this man, and have prayed about it, that's all that matters. You haven't known him very long, but time is of relative unimportance, if you are meant for each other. Your Aunt Martha married a man nine years younger you know, and they are very happy after many years."

"I didn't know that! Rory's parents divorced and his father married an older woman, too."

"It happens more frequently than you might think. The important thing is your commitment to each other."

"I know we haven't known each other very long, but I feel I've known him forever. He's so kind, Mama, so considerate. He treats me like I'm special, and he listens to me as though I have something important to say. I'm not used to that. It sounds silly at my age, but I feel like a princess in a fairy tale. I'm happier than I've ever been. It is so perfect that it frightens me a little." She paused for a long moment. "Do you think God brought us together?"

Catherine did not answer for some moments. Amanda waited impatiently, wanting a confirmation of her belief.

At last, her mother turned to her and said, "I don't know, Amanda, but I do know He turns bad things into good. I admit the events you've told me seem more than mere coincidence. I've been saying extra prayers for you and the children for the last few months, too, you know. They need a father, as well. Do you think Rory will be good for them?"

"He says he wants to take care of them, as well as me. He has a little boy, but he never gets to see him. He appears to enjoy being around David's children. I'm more concerned whether the children will accept Rory, I think."

"Follow your heart, Amanda, as well as your head. I do know that God answers prayer."

They became aware of raised whoops and howls of laughter. Rory, Matthew, and Joshua were tossing a football around in the backyard.

Amanda smiled, "Well, that's a start."

Catherine made a Mexican casserole for lunch and Amanda made a garden salad. She persuaded her mother to allow everyone to fill their own plates in the kitchen to save on washing up, so they could visit more. As they all gathered in the dining room for the blessing, Rory whispered in Amanda's ear.

"Do we help our plates?"

Amanda eyes him suspiciously. A joke, no doubt, but she decided to play along. "Help our plates do what?" she asked innocently.

Rory stared at her, obviously puzzled. "Do we help our plates? There is no food on the table, and no plates."

As understanding dawned, Amanda smothered her mirth by biting hard on her lip as Sue began the blessing. At "Amen," she ran out the kitchen door and exploded into laughter. Rory followed her, his face filled with concern. He stopped short when he heard the sounds erupting from her mouth. She grabbed him in a quick embrace, her laughter ebbing. "Darling Rory," she gasped, "I love you so much. You make me laugh," she added and gave him a kiss.

"I love you, too," he said uncertainly, "but what...."

"I'll explain later," she promised. "Let's go in and eat before someone comes to check on us."

After lunch, her brother, Ed, sister-in-law, Patricia, with their two boys, and her sister, Kate, husband, Jerry, and little boy, and Amanda's grandmother and maiden aunt arrived. It was a noisy, boisterous afternoon. Rory was the center of covert attention and he handled it well, she thought. He caught Amanda's eye on occasion, and they smiled at each other—he, as if to ask, Am I passing the test?, and she encouraging him and promising it wouldn't last forever. It did last for hours—through supper, which was hamburgers grilled outdoors, under elm trees that surrounded the area of house and barns. The setting sun filled the western sky with bands of violet, pink, and orange. The laughter, the smell of charcoal, the togetherness, turned the simple meal into a feast.

When the dishes were done, Amanda and Rory were able to get away and went for a walk.

"I told you I had a big family," Amanda teased, "and this isn't all—another sister lives away."

"I didn't believe you!" Rory said. He appeared a little overwhelmed.

They walked slowly, holding hands, the moon lighting the path between the elm trees. The breeze ruffled their hair and stirred the leaves, creating a kaleidoscope of moonlight and shadows.

"Your parents are great! I knew they would be—they raised

you," Rory said. "Matthew and Joshua are good kids and we had fun today, but Elizabeth wouldn't have much to do with me."

"She's rather shy," explained Amanda, "but she will soon get used to you. She has liked men better than women since she was a baby. These last months have been so hard on them, and there were separations before this that they had to contend with. It's a miracle they aren't totally insecure. They really enjoy being here this summer. I think they realize that belonging to a family is important. It's rather like a vacation for them, though, and they will be forced to face reality soon." She tried to speak lightly, but there was a hint of apprehension in her voice.

"I can never take their dad's place; I won't even try, but I'll love them and care for them. It will be all right, Amanda, I promise you."

"You are a very special person, Rory. Most men would quickly shy away from a woman with three young children. Are you sure you have no second thoughts now that you've actually met them?"

Rory stopped and turned to her. "No, sweetheart, no second thoughts at all. I love you, I want to marry you, and I want your kids."

Amanda smiled as he cradled her in his arms, and nestled her head against his chest. *This is truly where I want to be*, she thought. *I will make this work. I love this man and I am determined to make him happy, whatever it takes.*

When they returned, Kate cornered Amanda in the kitchen. "Why don't you and Rory, and Ed and Patricia, come to our house for awhile. We can play games, or something and all get to know Rory better. I've hardly had a chance to speak to him."

"I don't know, Kate, it sounds like fun. But what will Mama say?"

"She will probably like a little quiet time, herself. We can put Ed's kids down to sleep at my house, and Sue can manage yours. She's becoming an expert!"

"Well, I'd like to. I'll ask Rory, and then talk to Mama."

Rory liked the idea, and Catherine agreed. Amanda then spoke to her children. She felt a little guilty about leaving them. After all, she had traveled hours to see them, but she relished the idea of getting reacquainted with Kate and Ed. The children didn't appear to mind at all, as they were involved in some game which involved running from one side of the yard to the other. She caught them one by one as they ran by her, gave each a quick kiss and promised to see them in the morning. "They'll hardly miss me, and will be out as soon as their heads hit the pillow," she surmised ruefully. And she could depend on her father to bring them inside before someone ran into a tree.

At Kate's house, Patricia put her sons to bed in the guest room, and Amanda helped Kate pop corn and make drinks. The six of them sat in the living room talking and munching, until Kate put records on the stereo and said she would like to dance—that it had been ages since she and Jerry had danced. And they did dance, the three couples, for hours. Amanda was enjoying the evening more than she had thought was possible. She had never had the opportunity to spend time with her brother and sister since they were children. She felt almost like a teenager at a party.

Suddenly, Ed exclaimed that it was after eleven o'clock, and that they had to drive almost forty miles to get home. Amanda was aghast. Where had the time gone? Her parents usually went to bed after the ten o'clock news. They must be wondering where she was. Kate suggested that they all spend the night and leave early the next morning after breakfast. After a short discussion, they approved her plan, and Amanda would call Catherine, hoping she was not asleep, and let her know she and Rory would not be back tonight. When her sleepy mother answered the phone, Amanda, quickly and apologetically informed her and said she would see her in the morning.

Kate entered the living room with an armload of blankets, followed by Ed with pillows.

"Will you be comfortable enough on the floor? I have more blankets if you need them."

They made four pallets with the blankets and assured Kate they would survive, especially as they were all so tired. In the bathroom, Patricia and Amanda giggled as they brushed their teeth with their fingers, as best they could. When they returned, Rory beckoned to Amanda.

"Are you sure this is all right with your mother?" he asked her, with a worried frown on his face. "If I keep you out all night?"

Amanda smiled. "We're well chaperoned, Honey. It's okay."

Despite her assurance, Rory insisted on sleeping on the far pallet with Ed and Patricia between him and Amanda. Amanda felt so cherished, she could not go to sleep. She lay there in the darkness, hugging herself, for some time. It was so good to be alive!

The next morning, Rory and Amanda decided to leave immediately, not waiting to have breakfast. They told a sleepy-eyed Kate thank you and they would see her soon, and left.

They arrived at Amanda's parents, just as they were finishing breakfast. Catherine had decided to forego church this morning so they could talk, as Amanda and Rory planned to leave after an early lunch. The children finished eating and went outside and Amanda poured coffee for Rory and herself and they sat stiffly at the table with Catherine and James, prepared for a battery of questions, especially from James, who, to their surprise, began talking about Amanda. He related amusing tales of her childhood. Soon he and Rory were laughing and Amanda squirmed with embarrassment. She looked to her mother, hoping she would intervene, but Catherine sat smiling in quiet contemplation. *She must have talked to Daddy last night and told him everything I said yesterday*, thought Amanda. She looked from Catherine to James. They know each other so well, they don't always agree, but they always respect each other, and it's obvious they love each other. I've caught their secret looks. This is what

I want for Rory and me after we've been married as many years as they have. The sound of laughter broke into her thoughts. Daddy is having a ball, but I think it's time to change the subject, if I can—but what subject? She wracked her brain, discarding ideas as soon as they formed, as being too obviously contrived. When she heard her father begin the story of the Tom turkey chasing her, she determined to do something, as soon as she could gain their attention.

"Daddy, Rory worked with his dad at Redstone Arsenal. Rory, tell him about that."

James studied her, puzzled at being interrupted, and Amanda looked pleadingly at her mother for support.

"What did your father do at Redstone Arsenal, Rory?" Catherine came to the rescue.

"He had a construction contract on some of the support structures, and I worked as a laborer one summer," said Rory. He added details as James and Catherine asked questions.

Then the conversation turned to Rory and Amanda's plans. Her parents seemed satisfied and spoke their approval.

Amanda spent the rest of the morning talking and playing with her children. She told them about the rented house, described their bedrooms (curtain choices were red for the boys and pink for Elizabeth). They laughed at the antics of their cat, Tinker, being thrust into country life. Tinker was a full-grown male calico that had adopted the family several years ago. He had traveled with them through three moves, but this was perhaps his most exciting home.

"He doesn't like Butch much," said Matthew. Butch was James' dog.

"And he won't have anything to do with Grandma's cats," added Joshua.

"Jeanette says he's stuck-up, but I love him," said Elizabeth, and she kissed the fifteen-pound animal on the top of his head, almost spilling him out of her small lap.

Tinker purred contentedly and eyed Amanda as though to say, "These kids belong to me. Don't worry, I'll take care of them."

Amanda laughed and ruffled his fur. "Don't get too big for your britches!" she whispered into one ear. Tinker dismissed that nonsense by closing his eyes.

"Mama, can't you stay here? There's plenty of room. Sue is going to teach me to drive the pickup," said Matthew. "Jeanette is already learning, and I would like to stay—if you stayed, too."

"Me, too," said Joshua, "we can do lots of things here."

Amanda homed in on, "Driving! Don't you two do anything without Jeanette or Grandpa being right there—do you understand? Promise me!"

"We'll be careful, Mama, don't worry!" Matthew said, with a grown-up, serious look that caught at Amanda's heart. She realized that they were no longer babies.

She studied her healthy, growing offspring. Matthew—his head reached her nose now, light brown hair and piercing dark brown eyes, perhaps a little too mature for his years, a little solemn, not quite so trusting as his brother, always holding back a part of himself. Joshua—an inch or so shorter, dark hair and eyes, a little stockier than Matthew, and ready to take on the world, constantly vying for attention, and determined to keep up with his older brother in everything. Elizabeth—a little too dependent, but growing out of her tomboy phase. She would be a beauty. "They are so different, such individuals, and none of them look like me," she mused. But all three were tanned and pink-cheeked, and Amanda thanked God for them once again.

"I miss you so much," said Amanda, gathering all three inside her arms. "You are having fun, aren't you? Do you still want to stay here until school starts?"

There was a roar of yeses. "All right, that's settled," she said. "I'll call every few days and I'll be back before you know it. You can write to me, too, you know—little notes telling me what you're doing."

Then came the question Amanda had been anticipating, and had waited for the children to bring up. It caught her by surprise by its abruptness.

"Mama, is Rory going to be our Daddy now?"asked Elizabeth.

Amanda gathered her thoughts and sent out a prayer for wisdom. "You remember I told you about your daddy and me—we just had too many problems to stay together any more. We talked about all that before we left, didn't we?"

All three nodded.

"And I told you that your daddy and I love each one of you very much. That will never change. Grownups sometimes make mistakes and it is hard on their children, and they wish it hadn't happened. They don't want their children to be hurt—ever."

She waited for questions, but the children just looked at her with sober expressions on their faces. *I'm making it too complicated*, she thought.

She tried again. "So, we came here to make things better for us. I've rented a nice house for us, there's a backyard to play in, and a basement for when the weather is bad."

"But, Mama, what about Rory?" asked Joshua.

Amanda looked at her son and touched his hair. Trust Joshua to cut to the heart of the matter. "Okay, about Rory. He has asked me to marry him. He wants you three, too. He wants all of us to be a family."

"Would we have to call him Daddy?" asked Matthew. Amanda could see tears beginning to form in his eyes. She took his hands in hers.

"Matthew, Rory will not take your daddy's place. He knows he couldn't do that. We can talk about what you want to call him."

"He throws the football pretty good," said Joshua.

"He smells good," said Elizabeth, "but not like Daddy."

Amanda hugged each child and told them to think about what

she had told them. They would discuss it again.

"Mama, you told us you and daddy don't love each other any more...." Matthew's voice faltered.

Amanda cupped his chin in her left hand, lifting it so she could look into his eyes, and brushed the hair from his forehead.

"Matthew, it's true, your daddy and I don't love each other any more. But, Mama and Daddy love is not the same as the love we have for you and Joshua and Elizabeth. That kind of love never stops—never, do you understand? No matter what happens, I will *always* love you. You will *always* be my little boy. Nothing can change that." She took him in her arms. He clung to her, his strong young arms almost squeezing the breath from her. She fought back tears as she reached to include Joshua and Elizabeth in her embrace. At length, she released them and straightened her back.

"All right, troops. You're strong, you're tough—I've already seen that. Things will get better every day, and nothing can defeat you. Remember, Jesus is with you always, and when He's on your side, you always win! I want to see big smiles now, all around. That's good! Any more questions?"

They shook their heads.

"If you think of any later, write them down and ask me next time I call." She studied them for a moment. They appeared to be pacified. "Now, let's have hand inspection for lunch."

The children glanced at their hands.

"Oh, that's terrible. You'll have mud sandwiches." Amanda pretended to be horrified.

The children giggled and ran to wash.

After a quick lunch, Amanda hugged and kissed everyone while Rory thanked her parents for having him and hoped to see them again soon. He solemnly shook hands with Matthew and Joshua, who stared at their feet, looking embarrassed, and gave Elizabeth a quick hug, which she shyly returned.

"I'll see you soon, and I'll take good care of your mother," he told them.

Then amidst a few tears, and exaggerated waves, Amanda and Rory drove away.

11

Oh how great is thy goodness

(Psalm 31:19)

Rory and Amanda rode in silence for some time, content with frequent glances at each other, a squeeze of a hand, a smile. The radio played softly in the background. They inhabited a small world of their own, surrounded by joy and contentment

Amanda broke the silence. "The kids are very perceptive. They asked if we were going to get married. Actually, it was Elizabeth, and she asked if you were going to be their daddy."

"She did?" exclaimed Rory. "What did you say?"

"I told them you had asked me and left it at that for now. I tried to explain—not very well, I'm afraid—anyway, I told them to think about it. What do you think of them?"

"They're very bright and well-behaved. I had fun playing with Matthew and Joshua, and even Elizabeth thawed a little this morning. More than that, Amanda, they're yours, and I love everything about you, including your children. It will be okay. Don't worry."

Amanda sighed, "I hope so."

Rory squeezed her hand. "I promise."

Amanda squeezed back. *I believe him*, she thought, *he'll make it work.* They lapsed into private thoughts.

Later, they talked about her family. Amanda told Rory that he had impressed her mother. He told her he had had a long talk with her dad, that he was quite a guy, and that they understood each other. Rory then began to tell her more about his family.

"My parents divorced when I was eleven. I didn't see my dad much and Mom worked. My sister, Gloria, is four years older than me. I think Grandad influenced me more than anyone. He taught me a lot about doing the right thing—keeping your word, and don't charge anything (I didn't always listen to that very well!) You'll like him. My grandmother died a year ago and Mom lives with Grandad now. I didn't have much, growing up." He went on, "I started working after school when Dad left, at a gas station, and worked there through high school, and you know, I worked for Daddy one summer at Redstone Arsenal. We got to know each other better that summer. Then Vietnam...."

"You've done so many things. That's one reason I thought you were older, I think...."

Rory interrupted, "Don't bring that up again, Amanda. I don't want to talk about that any more—it's settled, okay?" He frowned at her.

"I'm sorry. I won't mention it again," she agreed.

He smiled and reached for his harmonica. "What would you like to hear?"

"Shenandoah" she said and settled further into the seat to relax and enjoy the familiar melody. He played for almost an hour, every tune they could think of that he could coax out of the instrument, and ended with "This Song's For You," glancing at Amanda as often as safety allowed while driving on the freeway.

Amanda smiled as she caught some of the glances. *I guess that's our song. Having him play just for me causes chills to run up and down my back. It's so exciting! I love everything about him, everything about my life now. It's gone from terrible to wonderful in just a few weeks. I can hardly believe it! Oh, thank You, Jesus, thank You, thank You!*

They stopped for a light supper when they reached the city; then Rory took her home. It had been a happy trip, but tiring. Rory helped bring her bags, including several filled with vegetables, into the living room. Their good night kiss held commitment and promise, as did their "I love you," and Rory left.

Amanda did a few necessary chores and then soaked in a hot bath while thoughts of the weekend ran through her mind. By the time the water cooled, she was nodding and she sleepily crept into her bed. "Abba, Father, I have so much to think over and talk about with You, but I am so tired. Please forgive me, but can it wait until tomorrow? I praise You for this weekend, and for the children You have given me, for my parents, and for Rory. Keep all of them safe and close to You, in the name of Jesus. Amen."

12

He will be our guide

(Psalm 48:14)

The next Saturday, Amanda arranged a piece of driftwood, that she had found years ago and had taken with her on several moves, with a few rocks and some mounds of silver artemisia and white alyssum in front of the picture window. She planted purple and pink petunias and white Dianthus on each side.

Rory arrived and began to mow the grass and edge the walks, while she was working in the flower bed. He was setting up the sprinkler when Amanda stepped back on the lawn intent on inspecting her handiwork. Suddenly, she was being sprayed with cold water and she yelped in dismay, as she tried to cover her hair with her hands. She ran to the porch and glared at a grinning Rory kneeling by the outside faucet.

"You never know when it might rain!" he said.

"You … you … " she sputtered, and then realizing how much fun he was having, she had to grin, too. "You're incorrigible," she told him. "Come tell me how this looks," she commanded, pointing to the flowers, "and no more tricks!"

They walked to the center of the lawn, and Rory said, "It looks nice. Where did you get the driftwood?"

"I've had it a long time."

Rory stared at her. "You actually brought that thing on the moving van?"

Amanda was taken aback. She hadn't given it much thought at the time, but in retrospect, "It was rather foolish, wasn't it? I didn't want to part with it, and I really didn't think. I had to sell a lot of things. It was a silly thing to do."

"Well, maybe a little silly." he smiled. "But it was worth it. It looks great." He wiped a streak of mud off her nose. "You are so cute."

She went inside to dry off and fix lunch, while he finished the watering.

They ate lunch, folded laundry, vacuumed, and scrubbed. Rory insisted he wanted to help and Amanda was happy to oblige. In mid-afternoon, Rory packed his laundry and went home, while Amanda did some ironing and got dressed for their evening. They went to a new Mexican restaurant and then to a movie.

Sunday morning, Rory went to church with her for the first time, though she had asked him before. Rory listened attentively and told Amanda he was impressed with the minister.

Amanda sat on the couch on Friday after work, reading letters from the children. She glanced at her watch. It was unusual for Rory to be late. They were to go to dinner. Idly, she wondered if he had to work late. It had happened once before. He had told her that occasionally he might have to take care of something at night or on a weekend. No, he would have called her. She brushed worry away and returned to her letters.

Suddenly, the door opened and Rory entered, shutting the door firmly behind him. His face was strange. She couldn't identify the emotion it portrayed. She started to rise.

"Don't open the door. Don't look out the window," Rory cautioned. He silently took her arm and led her into the kitchen.

She stared at him, puzzled, "What...."

"There's a guy out there in his car. He'll go away in a few minutes."

"What guy? What's he doing?" she exclaimed.

"Ssh! Just a guy. Don't worry about it," Rory said, sheepishly.

"Rory! What's going on?" she demanded.

"All right," Rory said harshly. "This guy ran a stop sign and almost hit me. I yelled at him, and ... well, I shook my fist at him, too. He yelled obscenities at me and he's been tailing me all over town—right on my bumper. I could see him yelling in the rearview mirror. I drove around for a long time trying to lose him, but he stayed right behind me. Finally, I got through a light on yellow and I thought I had lost him. But when I got out of the car, he was back, and he parked out front."

Amanda gaped at him, speechless.

"He'll go away soon." Rory assured her.

"We should call the police!"

"No, no, honey. He'll cool down and leave in a minute." Rory walked to the window, pushed the curtain aside an inch or so and peered out into the darkness.

"What's he doing?" asked Amanda.

"Just sitting there. The idiot! It was his fault, not mine."

Amanda sat on a kitchen chair. She did not know what to do. Rory kept watch at the window.

"There, he's leaving now." Rory dropped the curtain back into place and turned to Amanda. He smiled. "It's okay now. He's gone. Are you ready to go eat?"

"Rory, what if he comes back later? He probably thinks you live here!"

Concern filled Rory's face. "I never thought of that! I don't think he'll come back, but maybe I should stay here for a couple of nights...."

"You can't do that!" Amanda interrupted.

"Just to watch over you, I mean! Just in case...." He frowned in thought. "If my car isn't here, he won't bother you, so we'll use your car for a few days. And you keep the door locked at all times. Don't open it unless you know who is there." He looked at her with concern. "I'm sorry, Honey, I shouldn't have lost my temper—but I just yelled at him and shook my fist You wouldn't think he would go crazy over that, when he was at fault." Rory took Amanda in his arms. "It will be okay. If he comes back, call me. I'll be here in ten minutes." He kissed her. "I'm so sorry, I never thought about this affecting you."

He looked so woe-be-gone, and Amanda was sure he was right, the man would not be back. "It's okay. Let's forget about it."

"Good! Get your purse, I'm hungry."

Amanda shook her head. "Being with you is an adventure," she said, smiling. "Yes, let's go. I'm hungry, too," she added, suddenly realizing that it was true.

A delicious meal followed by a drive in the foothills removed all traces of the incident from their minds. In fact, nothing seemed to mar their happiness in being together. They were watchful for the next few days, but the man did not reappear.

Amanda and Rory spent some enjoyable evenings with David and Debbie, had picnics in the mountains on weekend afternoons, and continued to go to church together on Sunday mornings. The next few weeks passed quickly.

Amanda spoke with her children once a week on the phone. They kept her informed on the garden's progress, frequently complaining that weeding was not their favorite chore, how the calves were growing and would eat from their hands. Jeanette had run the pickup into the side of a granary (little damage) and they were forbidden to drive for awhile (Grandpa had yelled some). Tinker and Butch still avoided each other, and a dozen other things.

They asked about Rory, but had no specific questions and Amanda didn't push it. She, in turn, told them about the curtains she had finished and hung in their bedrooms, the flowers she had planted, the picnics, and things Anne and Sarah had been doing.

Matthew had a birthday in the middle of August, and Amanda could not afford to make the trip to be with him, as she would be there in two weeks to bring them home. She mailed his present and talked to him on the phone. Grandma had made him a chocolate cake. There was chocolate ice cream, and his favorite spaghetti for the birthday dinner. Amanda cried after she hung up. She had never missed a child's birthday and vowed it would not happen again.

One Saturday they had finished the usual yard work and were enjoying a lunch of grilled cheese sandwiches and dill pickles, when Rory exclaimed: "I forgot to bring the present I found for you yesterday!"

Amanda begged him to tell her what it was, but he insisted she had to wait until he gave it to her.

"Finish your sandwich and we'll go get it. You've never seen my place—it's pretty small. The guy I share it with isn't there today, but it's a mess. I have to clean it this afternoon."

"I'll help—you always help me. Do you have all the cleaning supplies?"

"Of course! I *do* clean it once in awhile!"

They drove to the little house on the west side. Amanda walked into the living room. The furniture was nice, French provincial. Rory said most of it was his. She noticed a work table in one corner held several items that she thought had something to do with electronics—radios or such. She walked over to take a closer look, and Rory proudly explained.

"This is sort of a hobby. Actually, I started a home-study course in electronics, and some of this I built for that."

He turned dials and switches and one box lit up with a green screen. Lines began to move across the screen in different configurations as he turned dials. Amanda was spellbound.

"What is it?" she whispered.

"It's an oscilloscope. What you see is an electrical wave."

"I know almost nothing about physics; but this is fascinating."

He turned dials and Amanda watched the lines on the screen move into different shapes for several minutes. Finally, she forced her attention away from the screen.

"We had better get the cleaning done," she said reluctantly.

Rory led her into the kitchen. There were the usual appliances and a kitchen table with four chairs. It did not look too dirty—wash a few dishes and sweep the floor and it would be presentable. In fact, Amanda thought the house was exceptionally clean for two guys living in it. She walked over to the range.

"What is this, Rory?" she asked, pointing to a skillet containing drying remains of a gluey green substance she could not identify. A saucepan held a small amount of what looked like rice, but it also was green.

Rory looked at the skillet. "It's gravy," he said. It was my turn to cook last night and I fixed fish with rice and gravy."

"But it's green! And the rice! I've never seen rice like that before."

Rory laughed. "It looked sort of blah, so I added some food coloring. It tasted pretty good!" he insisted, seeing the look on her face.

Amanda was speechless.

"It was good!" Rory repeated. "Bob liked it, too."

Amanda took her eyes away from the pans. "I'll take your word for it! But why green? Why not yellow, or even pink?"

"Green was all I had," he admitted.

Amanda laughed. "I'll clean up the kitchen."

Rory demurred, but she insisted and he left to scrub the bathroom.

Amanda shook her head and began to fill the sink with hot water. She scraped the contents of the skillet and pan into a bag, and put the bag in the wastebasket. There were few dirty dishes, and she quickly washed plates, glasses, forks, etc., and put the skillet in the hot soapy water to soak for a few minutes while she wiped counters, table and stove top. The skillet residue responded to a few strong swipes with a scouring pad. As she finished and was drying her hands, she called to Rory, "Say, where is my present?"

"Be with you in a minute," he called back.

She walked to the window and stood looking out on a small, grassy yard with a couple of pine trees along one end. A hedge nearly hid the house next door. A quiet neighborhood, in an older part of town, near the foothills. *Very charming*, thought Amanda. She thought it significant that Rory chose to live here rather than in a modern apartment. She turned as she sensed him behind her.

"It's nothing, really, but I thought of you when I saw it." He handed her a small package. "I thought you might like it. I found it in a junk shop."

Amanda carefully unfolded the wrapping. Inside was a small china bowl, and perched on the side was a tiny figure of a girl in a long, full dress, with her knees drawn up. One hand was under her chin and she appeared to be in deep thought. It looked very old.

"It's exquisite!" breathed Amanda. "I love it. It's so delicate, almost ethereal."

"I thought she looked a little like you—tiny and so serious. I'm not quite sure you're real, either, when I'm away from you." He drew her into his arms. "Am I imagining you?"

"No," she whispered, pulling his face down to hers. They sank to their knees. After a few moments, Rory pushed her away.

"We had better get out of here. Come on, I'll take you home," he said shakily.

She got to her feet, snatched her purse, and went to the car. They sat silently as Rory drove with savage ferocity, as though they were being pursued by evil. Amanda sat stiffly, holding onto the door handle as they swung around corners. They did not look at each other.

"We have to talk about this. I didn't want to leave," he said hoarsely.

"Yes, I know. Neither did I," she whispered.

Rory sighed and slowed to a safer speed.

"It's a long time until we can marry you know," Amanda said and dared to glance quickly at him. His face was flushed and his mouth was set in a firm line. She continued, "You are very special—very strong—thank you."

His face softened. "We must be careful not to put ourselves into a situation like that again. You understand?"

"Yes, I know. We'll be very careful. I want everything to be just right—always." After a few moments she added, "The children will be here soon, and that will help."

Rory continued to drive with deliberation, not speaking or looking at Amanda.

Is he angry with me? she wondered. *This is my fault. I should have seen the danger. Father in heaven,* she prayed, *forgive me. Help us now, please. We want to do what is right.* She looked at Rory again. *I wonder what he would think if....*

Rory pulled into the driveway and shut off the engine. They sat quietly.

At last Amanda broke the long silence. "Rory, I think perhaps we should pray about this—together." She looked at him, he was staring straight ahead at nothing. "What do you think?"

Rory turned to her, a mystified look on his face. "Pray? About this? Do you think God will help us with this, too?" he asked, skeptically.

Amanda swallowed and looked at her hands as they twisted and untwisted in her lap. She spoke slowly, searching for the right words. "We believe He brought us together. We know He loves us and wants what's best for us. So wouldn't He listen to us now? He is the model for an earthly father—fathers listen to their children and want to give them good things. Sometimes fathers say no, if something is not good for their child. I believe God does the same." She looked at Rory. "Jesus knew about temptation," she added, again studying her hands.

"I never thought about it quite like that," he said slowly. "It makes God more real—as a father would be." He looked at her searchingly, "You really believe what you said." It was a statement, not a question. "I can tell that you do."

"Yes, I believe it. I would probably not have made it through the months before I came here without that belief and without prayer about many different things."

Rory sat, frozen, his hands gripping the steering wheel, a frown of deep concentration on his face. Amanda waited. At last he faced her.

"Can we go inside? I think we should pray, as you said, but not out here. I've never prayed with anyone like this before. I don't know how."

Amanda opened her door, found her key and they went inside. She took her Bible from the side table and sat on the couch. Rory sat beside her.

"I've never prayed with anyone like this before either," confessed Amanda, "but … I'll start, then you can add whatever you wish." She placed her right hand on her Bible and took Rory's hand in her left and closed her eyes.

"Abba, Father, we believe that You hear us and that You answer when we call. We need Your help, Father.…" She asked God to give them guidance and strength and to bless their relationship. She paused, eyes still closed. After a few seconds when Rory did not speak, she ended the prayer. " Thank You for caring for us as a Father cares for His children, in the name of Jesus. Amen."

Rory repeated, "Amen."

Amanda squeezed his hand, released it, and turned to him. He sat, arms on his legs, his hands clasped between his knees, his eyes on the floor. She waited.

"What does *Abba* mean?" he asked, still looking down.

"It's what a child would call his dad. An intimate, yet respectful name for your dad."

Rory did not move. "Amanda," he said at last, "You've shown me things I've never thought of before. I've had a picture in my mind of God as an old, white-haired, stern school master sort of God. I want to go home and think about this." He stood, "I'll see you later. We'll have dinner—about seven?"

She nodded and he kissed her lightly and left. She was spent and lay back on the couch and closed her eyes. In minutes she was asleep. She awoke about six with a headache, but at peace. She swallowed aspirin, drinking several glasses of water while standing at the bathroom basin. Her face was pale, with bright pink spots on her cheeks, and her eyes looked puffy. She considered calling Rory and canceling their date, but she wanted to know what had happened when he got home. He would need to talk about it, too, she decided. So she ran water in the tub, and added extra bubble bath. After soaking as long as she dared, she dressed carefully in her brightest dress. When she checked herself in the mirror, she was gratified. The hot, humid water had put extra curl in her hair, her eyes were clear, and the rose-colored flowers in her dress were reflected in her face. She was ready.

When Rory arrived, they smiled at each other and he held her hand for a moment or so before leading her to the car. She sat close to him, her hand resting lightly on his knee, but they did not speak. Amanda sensed that they had moved into a more precious dimension in their relationship.

They ate in a small seafood restaurant that was becoming a favorite place, keeping the conversation light and hardly noticing what they ate, until coffee was set before them. Then Rory reached across the table and took Amanda's hand in his.

"I went home to think, and I confess I was a little dubious about praying like we did. At the same time, I really wanted to believe like you do. I just sat for awhile. Then I got the Bible out. I didn't know where to start, although I've read most of it, and knew all the Sunday School stories. I read some Psalms and about Jesus feeding the multitude with a few fish. All the time I was reading, it was almost like being there. I thought, for the first time—I thought, I am reading about real people and these things are happening to them in their every-day lives—and God is making things happen. I began to understand what you meant. If God is our Father, He will act as a father on earth acts with his children." He smiled at Amanda. "You've shown me something very important—one more reason to love you." He stopped for a moment. "Enough serious talk. I feel so good! I want to tell everyone here about us, and that God loves us."

Happiness consumed Amanda and she laughed aloud.

They finished their coffee and drove to her house. At the door, Rory held her. "I'll leave you here. I'll pick you up in the morning for church."

Amanda kissed his check. "Wonderful. We'll decide together if this church is right for us."

Rory kissed her very tenderly and Amanda went inside. She danced around the room as she got ready for bed, almost bursting with happiness. "Thank You, Father, thank You Jesus, thank You Holy Spirit, for this day. Thank You for this man. Thank You for loving me."

A week before they were to pick up the children, Rory broached the subject of a visit to his family in Texas. They could make a quick trip over Labor Day weekend, he told her.

"The children, too?" Amanda asked.

"Of course—I want Mom and Grandad to meet them."

"It's a long trip with three children. How long will it take?"

"About fourteen hours. I thought we could drive straight through, get there sometime Saturday morning and leave Monday morning."

"Did your Mom invite us? What does she say about us?"

"She wants to meet you. I don't know if she believes what I've told her about you. She wants to see for herself." He laughed. "She and my sister don't trust me to choose a nice girl," he added and winked at her.

Amanda returned a weak smile. "Tell me more about them. I can understand their concern—a divorcee with three children, quite a bit older."

"No!" Rory interrupted, "you promised."

"Sorry," she said contritely. "You know what I mean, though. They're probably very uneasy.,"

"Then we'll go and show them, all right?"

"I think it's a good idea, although I'm scared. What if they don't like me?"

"They will. You'll get along fine. And if by some chance they don't, that's their problem." Rory told her his mom lived with his grandad, a couple miles outside town. His grandad bought and sold cattle and they both loved to fish. His sister was married and had a little girl.

Amanda didn't think that told her much and she dreaded the meeting, but realized that it was necessary, and the sooner the better.

That Sunday, after church, Amanda and Rory went to her house for lunch. Rory turned on the TV and relaxed on the couch while Amanda went to the kitchen. Rory usually helped her with meals—he enjoyed experimenting with herbs and spices, but he had mentioned having a tough work-week. She always liked to prepare most of the Sunday dinner on Saturday, and she had a pot roast in the refrigerator. She placed it in the oven to heat and made a salad. She would fill the plates in the kitchen, she decided, so she selected cutlery and napkins for the table. She noticed that Rory was lying on the sofa with his legs curled up. He had apparently fallen asleep. She turned the burner on low, took an afghan from the closet and draped it over his legs, and curled up in the chair with a book.

After about twenty minutes, she turned the burner off under the roast, fearing it would be overcooked and dry. Rory slept on. Finally, at two o'clock, she decided to wake him. She stood over him and gently shook his arm. Rory moaned and his arms shot out striking Amanda. She sat down hard on the floor, incredulous, and blinking back tears of pain.

Rory sat up. "Amanda! Honey, are you all right?" He picked her up and sat with her on his knees. "I'm sorry, sweetheart! Are you hurt?"

"No-o, I'm okay. What happened?"

"I should have warned you. Since Vietnam … it's reflex, if I get woken up suddenly. Are you sure you're all right?"

She assured him she was and he began to talk about Vietnam, for the first time since they had met. He had told her he was in Vietnam, and that was all, no details. He talked now—the words spilling one over another—of nights in the jungle … of the silence, and of the fear … of guard duty in the black unknown … of being weary and unable to sleep in huts where the Viet Cong would often infiltrate the camp, silently kill a sleeping soldier in his bunk and steal away in the night. Amanda listened in horror.

"Even yet," he said and hugged her tighter, "if something wakes me out of sound sleep…." He squeezed her to him. "I wouldn't hurt you …" he said, with tears in his eyes.

"I know, Sweetheart; I know you wouldn't hurt me," Amanda cradled his head on her shoulder. "I'm so sorry you went through that." Tears ran down her cheeks. "Oh, Sweetheart, how horrible. I didn't know!"

They held each other for a long time. Rory seemed lost in a nightmare of the past and Amanda tried to imagine what his thoughts were, but she knew this part of his life could never be shared openly with her. She could only pray that the dreadful memories would grow faint with time. At last Rory's eyes met hers, and she welcomed him back to her with a smile.

"I can't believe I hit you like that! Was it on your arm? Let me look."

"I don't know," Amanda answered in surprise. "My arm … and my shoulder, I think."

Rory gently probed both arms and shoulders. There was a little tenderness, but no bruising was visible. Rory rubbed his face with one hand, distressed by what he had done.

Amanda pulled his hand away from his face and kissed him gently. "Please don't, Honey. It's okay. You're making me feel terrible." She touched his cheek and kissed him again. He gave her an apologetic smile. "Can we talk about something else now?" she asked, and her eyes pleaded with him to forget.

He nodded and kissed her on the cheek. "I love you."

Eventually, she reheated the roast. They ate little, but not because it was overcooked. Their thoughts were still on the tragedies of war, even though they spoke about mundane events and occurrences and tried to cheer each other. It was several hours before they returned to their usual gaiety.

On Wednesday evening, they had their supper of crab salad and French bread in the living room. The television was on and they watched it desultorily while discussing their trip to collect the children that weekend.

"I have to register them for school soon, too. I hope I have all the records I need.

"I have to register, too," said Rory.

"Register? For what?" Amanda asked curiously.

"I'm working on an associates degree in business. GI Bill, you know?"

"You hadn't told me! I think that's wonderful! You go to night classes?"

"Yes, four nights a week, 7:00 to 10:00. I hadn't mentioned it because I thought you might not like it. I don't much like it either, but…."

"I don't understand. What do you mean?"

"I won't be able to see you as much. We can't go out. Ten o'clock is too late."

"Rory! I thought you knew me better than that! I'm very happy you're working on a business degree. That's great! I'm proud of you. It's tough going to school at night."

"You aren't upset?"

"Of course not! I'll miss seeing you every evening, and I know you'll have to study, but we'll have weekends. How far along are you?"

"I'm about half-way through, I guess."

"That's wonderful! I can't believe you hadn't told me!"

She squeezed his arm, tilting her plate, and her fork fell to the floor, taking crab pieces with it. Rory had finished eating by the time Amanda cleaned up the mess, and they returned to the subject of their trip. They planned to leave very early Saturday morning and return the same evening.

13

In quietness and in confidence shall be your strength

(Isaiah 30:15)

Rory arrived before sunrise on Saturday, and Amanda was ready. She was eager to have her children with her. She picked up a thermos of coffee and some fruit and crackers to snack on and stepped into the car.

The first sun rays were gilding the tops of the mountains. And the air was cool and refreshing. It would be a lovely day for traveling. Amanda relaxed against the seat and went over her preparations, in her mind, hoping she hadn't forgotten anything. Rory fiddled with the radio and found a station playing soft popular music.

Soon they had left the city and most of the traffic behind, and the double rows of asphalt rose and fell before them, nearly due south. As the sun rose into the sky, the temperature rose inside the car, and they lowered the windows, creating a welcome draft, and a not-so-welcome noise, as the wind rushed through the openings. Rory increased the volume on the radio. After a few minutes, he switched it off and reached for his harmonica. Amanda closed her eyes and her mind to all distractions and allowed herself to become captivated by Rory's music.

He played "Amazing Grace" and other hymns, snatches of Beethoven, her favorite "Shenandoah," and their song. The miles and the hours slid by. The car was infused with the pleasure of their being together.

They arrived at the farm just before lunch, having crossed a time zone and losing an hour. Catherine was dumbfounded at their plans to start back in a couple of hours. Amanda apologized for not making that clear on the phone the day before, and spent a few minutes convincing her mother that she needed the next day to help the children adapt to their new home before she went to work on Monday.

So after devouring the meat loaf Catherine had prepared, they were ready to pack the car. Amanda stepped out the back door, carrying some of the children's bags and stared in disbelief at the accumulation the children had heaped at the rear of the station wagon, where Rory stood in bewilderment.

"What is all that?" Amanda demanded.

"It's our stuff," said Matthew, dropping another armful to the ground and looking innocently at his mother.

"You … we … but …" Amanda sputtered to a halt, dropping the bags from her hands. She strode to the nearest pile and began checking the contents of bags, boxes, and buckets. Most she stacked to one side, while the children jumped around her, wailing.

"Those are special rocks!" cried Matthew, as Amanda hefted a bucket to the 'No' pile.

"Pick out five, only five—small ones," his mother commanded.

"Mama, Grandpa gave me those deer antlers. I want to hang them in my room!" Joshua pleaded. Amanda looked at her son's tears, and relented, with some misgiving.

"No, Mama, please!" whimpered Elizabeth, reaching for a bag Amanda was about to toss aside.

"Elizabeth, what is this stuff?" asked Amanda, as she peered into the bag.

Elizabeth carefully reached in and began pulling out her treasures. "This is a bird nest, it blew out of the tree over there, but there were no eggs in it," she said, pointing to a huge cottonwood. "This is a rabbit's foot that I found in the cellar. It used to be Uncle David's. Grandpa said I could have it. And these are caterpillars," she said proudly, holding up a glass jar with holes punched in the lid, and wilted leaves covering the bottom. Mother and daughter peered at the jar, their heads touching.

"I can't see them, Mama, what happened to them?" Elizabeth asked , looking at her mother.

Amanda put an arm around her daughter. "Sweetie, the caterpillars couldn't survive in the jar for very long, without great care. You know that; we've talked about it before. Wild things need to be free. It is really not fair to pen them up."

A tear slid down Elizabeth's check. "I know. They were so pretty—yellow stripes around them. I wanted to keep them, but I forgot about them. I found a toad, too, but I let it go." She looked at her mother for approval.

"That was good, Elizabeth." Amanda gave her a hug.

"Can I keep the wild flowers? I picked them in the pasture and Sue helped me press them in a book.

"Yes, all right, that was nice of Sue. Are they in this box?"

Elizabeth nodded and Amanda put the box in the 'okay' pile.

Eventually, everything was sorted out, leaving more than half of the original to be left behind.

Amanda ran her hands through her hair. "Okay, kids. All this stuff has to be put away," she pointed at the discards, "before Grandpa sees the mess. Figure out where it belongs and do a neat job."

The children reluctantly picked up items and walked off in different directions. Amanda looked at Rory, who had been standing patiently by the car. "I wonder if he knows what he is letting himself in for," she murmured to herself. He smiled encouragingly.

"Do you think the rest of this will fit into the car?" she asked.

He assured her it would and picked up a box. Amanda sighed. In no time, Rory had transferred the treasures to the safety of the cargo area.

"Mama, we forgot about Tinker!" exclaimed Matthew.

"Oh my!" Amanda's shoulders slumped. "Where is he, and where is his carrier?" she asked.

The children ran to find him—no easy task. Tinker was a seasoned traveler, having moved three times, and he knew the signs well. Rather than submit to the indignity of being confined in his carrier, he had disappeared.

He was eventually found, a good half hour later, behind a stack of empty feed sacks in a granary.

Joshua yelled and attempted to pick him up, but was cowed by a Tinker who, in desperation, emitted a fair imitation of a Great Dane. Amanda arrived, and being in no mood for *catrionics*, grabbed the creature by the scruff of his neck, and ignoring his piteous meows, stuffed him into the carrier, which Matthew had brought to the scene.

At last, following lengthy farewells and a few tears, the children were coaxed into the back seat, Amanda and Rory in front, and the laden station wagon moved slowly down the drive. The children sat soberly in the back seat, uncertain what their future would be like. In a short time, however, they had dismissed vague fears, as the natural resiliency of children everywhere (and these three were seasoned travelers as well) took over. They talked among themselves for awhile, keeping a wary eye on Rory. They played games Amanda had taught them on earlier journeys and occasionally commented on the countryside they were speeding through. Amanda passed out cookies and grapes, and there was an inevitable rest stop. The afternoon waned and the children became restless, bickering with each other. Amanda turned to admonish them, telling them to be quiet and it would not be very much longer. Rory stretched his head to look in the rear view mirror, and eyed the three stony little faces.

He began to recite in a deep voice.

> *"Hickory, dickory, dock,*
> *The mouse ran up the clock.*
> *The clock struck one,*
> *But all the rest escaped with minor injuries."*

After a short silence, Elizabeth (seated between her brothers to prevent arm wrestling and other physical games) giggled.

"What's so funny?" muttered Matthew, still in a funk.

"That's not right!" exclaimed Elizabeth.

Joshua's eyes suddenly brightened, and he studied the back of Rory's head with interest. "How did it go? Say it again," he demanded.

Rory did so, with Joshua repeating each line after him. A big smile creased his face.

"Oh, I get it," said Matthew, feigning boredom, but he sat up straighter in anticipation.

"Tell us another one," begged Elizabeth.

> *"Little Miss Muffet sat on her tuffet,*
> *Eating her curds and whey.*
> *Along came a spider and sat down beside her,*
> *And said, 'Hey, good lookin, what you got in the bowl?'"*

Elizabeth and Joshua squealed with laughter. Even Matthew chuckled. Rory continued to regale them with nonsense verses until they neared the city.

He ended with: "Did you know that, Humpty Dumpty was a big yolk?"

Finally, they arrived safely at their new home. The children wanted to explore immediately, but Amanda insisted that the car be unpacked first. The first chore was to take the cat carrier, containing a sleeping Tinker, to the basement, where he would not be able to get loose and become lost in new surroundings. Amanda handed the carrier to Matthew, with full instructions and dispatched Joshua and Elizabeth to find his dish and fill it with food and fresh water. They were then to provide him with a litter box. A packing box would serve temporarily, as the ancient pan previously used was discarded when they moved, and Tinker had stayed outdoors at the farm.

Then, amid mild protests, muted at Amanda's stern look, the neatly packed items in the car became a disorganized mass on the living room floor. Amanda eyed this speculatively, but, after a moment's thought, wisely dismissed the children and they raced around the house while Amanda went to the kitchen to make coffee, and Rory searched for his bag which had unaccountably been removed from the car.

Amanda sank into a chair, happy to be home with her children. She wondered, idly, if she could find clothes suitable for church in the morning, and was grateful she had Sunday afternoon to get organized. When the coffee was ready, she brought mugs to the living room, and, pushing bundles out of her path with her foot, handed one to Rory. They sat, tired but smiling, surrounded by clutter.

The hot liquid soon revived their flagging energy, and by the time the children returned, enthusiastic and full of questions, they were almost ready for them.

They approved the curtains and the boys asked if they could rearrange furniture in the room they shared. Amanda agreed with some reservations, and Rory went to help with the heavier things. Elizabeth prattled happily, while Amanda helped her put her things away. Tinker, released from the basement now that the front door was safely closed, took possession of Elizabeth's bed and glared at them each time they jostled against it.

Rory took Matthew and Joshua with him to pick up a pizza while Amanda made a salad and iced tea, and Elizabeth set the table.

"Will Rory sit here?" asked Elizabeth, pointing to the head of the table.

Amanda hesitated, realizing the implication. *Lord, help me!* she prayed quickly. "I guess so, Elizabeth, and we can sit as we used to: you on this side, Matthew and Joshua on the other, and I'll sit here nearest the kitchen. Is that okay?"

"Sure,"said Elizabeth, as she placed napkins at each place. "I'll sit at this end by Rory."

Amanda smiled happily.

Supper was lively. The children told more stories about their summer. Their mirth turned to groans when Amanda mentioned that school would be starting and that they had to register.

"A new school, and we don't know anybody," they lamented.

Amanda sympathized. "I know, but you'll make friends soon. You've done this before. You're experts by now," she spoke lightly, but inside she ached for them. *Be with them, Jesus,* she prayed. "We'll drive by your schools tomorrow. They aren't far. Now, time for baths and lay out clothes for church in the morning. If you need help, let me know. Scoot!"

Amanda and Rory lingered at the table over coffee.

"I'll have to get used to all that energy," Rory said with a grin. "I'm worn out, and had better get home." He added, "See you in the morning."

Amanda tucked in the children and heard their prayers. Each child, without a word from her, added Rory's name to their 'God bless …' list, which touched her heart. They went to sleep easily, obviously enjoying their own rooms, even though they were in a different location. Too, they were undoubtedly exhausted after such a busy day.

Sunday, after church, Rory asked the children if they would like to go to a cafeteria for dinner, and (no surprise), they exuberantly said yes. Amanda protested, thinking it too expensive, but Rory insisted it wasn't a problem. *He's forgotten how growing boys eat!* she thought, and against her better judgment, she gave in. She told the children to choose carefully as she spotted the long counter filled with hundreds of choices. Rory told them to get anything they wanted and they eagerly got their trays and started down the line. Amanda shuddered, *He'll soon learn—the hard way!*

The boys' trays were so full that an attendant had to help them carry them to a table. Elizabeth's tray was lighter, but consisted of dishes of fried chicken and desserts—no veggies, except a huge corn on the cob.

Rory looked a little pale when Amanda stole a glance at him as he stood waiting for the cashier to total the bill. However, he smiled gamely as he paid it. Amanda bit her lower lip to keep from saying, "I tried to tell you," and walked toward the table. There were so many dishes surrounding Matthew and Joshua, that she chose the next table for Rory, Elizabeth, and herself.

"Just wait until we get home, you little barbarians!" she whispered to the boys as she walked by.

She was so embarrassed that the food stuck in her throat. Rory, apparently, had fully recovered and chatted with Elizabeth as they began eating heartily after the blessing by Matthew. They soon noticed Amanda was very quiet and was pushing her food around with her fork.

"Aren't you hungry, Mama? Do you have a stomach ache?" asked Elizabeth.

"What's wrong, Honey?" asked Rory.

"I guess I'm not very hungry—it's quite good though," Amanda said, and made an effort to eat. The three of them finished and sat with their drinks, waiting for Matthew and Joshua.

Finally, they had to give it up. They could not finish all the food, although they made a good fight of it! Now they looked at their mother and noticed her face. There were tiny lines around her tight mouth, and that was a sure sign of impending doom.

On the way home they passed a multi-flavors ice cream shop, and Rory teasingly asked the children if they would like ice cream. He received groans in answer, and laughed. Amanda, however, didn't crack a smile, and, noticing her distress, Rory grasped her hand to let her know everything was fine.

At the house, Amanda told the children to change to play clothes, and two sober-faced little boys went straight to their room without protest.

Rory chose a Ferrante & Teicher album from Amanda's collection and made himself comfortable on the couch. Amanda sat beside him and he took her hand.

"I know what you're thinking. Don't be too rough on them."

"They must begin learning to make good decisions."

"I think they learned something today."

"Would you let me pay you back for some of that food?" she asked, and added menacingly, "I may take it out of their allowance!"

"Don't be silly. I'm just glad I cashed a check yesterday. We'll have light dates this week," he said and winked at her.

"You're very sweet and understanding. I didn't want us to get started like this!"

"Forget it, we're starting out fine."

"Excuse me for a minute," said Amanda and she went to the boys' room. They were sitting on their bed, eyes downcast.

Amanda quashed a wry smile and arranged a stern look on her face. "You both know what I will say, don't you?"

They nodded, not looking at her.

"Look at me, please." They reluctantly raised their eyes. She continued, "I won't say it, then, but I believe you owe Rory an apology, don't you?"

They nodded again and slowly stood up and walked past her to the living room. They told Rory they were sorry that they had acted like pigs and promised not to do it again. Joshua added, "Anyway, we don't feel so good."

"It's okay, guys, we all make mistakes," said Rory, trying not to smile, "Let's forget it."

"Yes, Sir," said Matthew. "Yes, Sir," echoed Joshua.

"Good! If your mother agrees, how would you like to go to the park and work off some of that food?"

Both boys smiled and looked at their mother.

Amanda nodded in agreement and Rory left to change clothes, promising to be back in half an hour. Amanda helped Elizabeth hang up her dress and then went to change into jeans and cotton shirt.

At the park, they played a version of touch football, with Elizabeth mostly in the role of cheerleader. At one point, Amanda was chasing Matthew, who had the ball. Matthew turned suddenly, crashing into Amanda. She lost her footing and fell in a muddy area with a few sprigs of grass. Her face banged against the ground. The children whooped with laughter at the sight of their mother wiping mud off her arms and face and trying to brush her jeans clean. Rory had a twinkle in his eye, but he managed to stifle his laughter. Amanda made a face at them and promised revenge. She played more aggressively, having decided that her sons were almost as big as she was, and a good deal tougher. It was nearly dark when Rory drove them home.

"I won't come in...." Rory stopped and stared at Amanda. "I think your eye is turning black!"

"What?" Amanda pulled down the sun visor and examined her face. "Oh, no!" How am I going to explain this?" she moaned.

She looked at Rory. He was struggling to keep a straight face, as were the three in the back. Her look of distress changed into a smile. "Just wait until next time; I'll fix all of you!"

Giggles erupted from the back seat and Rory laughed and kissed her gently on the nose. "I've never kissed a girl with a black eye," he teased.

"Oh you!" she retorted and slapped his arm away.

"I'll call you tomorrow. You might put some ice on that eye—I don't have enough money to go buy a steak!" Rory told her.

She gave him a withering look and got out of the car. The children followed, trying to hide their smirks.

Amanda supervised the children's baths and put muddy clothes in the washer. She heated soup and they ate their light supper. The children were enthusiastic about their day and declared Rory "neat." They refrained from mentioning their mother's eye.

After the children were in bed, Amanda examined her face. There was a slight discoloration near the bridge of her nose and under her left eye, but only a hint of swelling. She wrapped an ice cube in a cloth and held it on the spot for several minutes. She couldn't see any improvement and went to bed hoping for the best. Her prayers were filled with thanksgiving that she had her children with her, and that, so far, they seemed to be accepting Rory. There was no mention, in her prayer, of the mortifying events at the cafeteria. The thought crossed her mind to ask Jesus to please let her children's manners improve, but she had promised Rory not to speak of it again, and she decided that included talking to the Lord. She did ask that her eye not be noticeably black by morning.

When she examined her face in the mirror the next morning, there was only a smudge of darkness near her eye. A little makeup took care of that. She got the children up and fed them and took them to Debbie on the way to work, reminding them to behave at Aunt Debbie's. Elizabeth was delighted to have two girl cousins to play with and the boys were well supplied with balls and games. Amanda hoped they could keep themselves entertained. It was a lot to ask of Debbie, even though Amanda insisted on paying her, there was no way that money would repay her kindness. At least school would start in two weeks.

That week passed quickly, with Rory and the children becoming better acquainted. Rory took no part in telling them what to do, or not to do, yet made it clear that he was more than a casual visitor. Amanda was a little surprised at his skill. He had not had much experience dealing with children. She walked with a spring in her step and her demeanor emanated confidence.

One evening as she walked down the hall to check on the children who were playing in Elizabeth's room, she heard Joshua say, "Mama was singing again in the kitchen after dinner."

"I had never heard Mama sing before, except in church," added Elizabeth.

"I remember—she used to," said Matthew, "a long time ago."

Amanda wiped her eyes and tiptoed away. But a few minutes later, as she dried the dishes, she was startled when she realized she was singing a popular song she had heard on the car radio.

14

Thy people shall be my people

(Ruth 1:16)

Rory, Amanda, and the children gathered in the living room one evening to discuss the trip to visit Rory's mother. They decided to leave Friday evening and drive straight through, with Amanda taking a turn at the wheel. They would leave very early Monday morning, Labor Day, to come home.

On Friday, they quickly packed the car. Small toys and games, along with pillows, were placed in the back seat. Amanda had a bag of snacks and a thermos of coffee as well as a small water jug at her feet. She pushed a pillow into the space between her and the door, and they were off.

They ate sandwiches and bananas that Amanda had prepared, looked for cars with out-of-state license plates, and played other on-the-road games until dark. Then Rory found his harmonica and began to play. At first there were a few smothered giggles from the back, but soon the children began to make requests for songs they knew.

Amanda leaned back in the seat and closed her eyes. Apprehension had plagued her for several days and now anxiety threatened to swamp her. She knew she and the children would be under close scrutiny. The barrier of a previous marriage, three children, plus the circumstance that she was never to talk about, might prove more than she could overcome. *Father, please let his family not pass judgment on us until they see that I'm committed to making Rory happy and that it will work out with the children. Give me wisdom to deal with this in the right way, and, please, help the children to be on their best behavior. Help me to make this a positive meeting. I feel Your blessing on us—You have taken us this far. Thank You, Father. I trust You to take me through this, too.* She forced herself to relax and enjoy the music.

The children gradually arranged themselves as comfortably as was possible in the seat, and fell asleep. Rory put his harmonica away and found a radio station playing soft music. The air became warmer as they traveled south, and the wind whistled through the half-open windows. Amanda hoped it would not be too hot. She did not feel well in hot, humid areas, and had suffered from heat exhaustion when she had lived on the Gulf coast.

At midnight, she awoke from a doze. As soon as her eyes would focus, she offered to drive for a while.

"I'm not tired, but I'll stop and get us some coffee," answered Rory.

They sipped the hot liquid and Rory talked about his childhood. He told her of living with his parents in a house near a small lake. They had a few ducks on the lake and, one by one, they began to disappear. He was fishing one morning and saw an alligator grab one of the remaining ducks, snapping off its legs. He ran to tell his dad, who didn't believe there was an alligator in the little pond. Finally, Rory persuaded him to take a look and they examined the duck. This was convincing evidence, and a few days later his dad shot the eight-foot alligator. No one knew how it got into the lake.

He spoke of frog gigging in the swamp at night and watching

for water moccasins that were prone to fall from overhead branches into their boat, being attracted by the torch lights. Amanda shivered. She hated snakes.

Once he and a friend decided to get rid of a tree stump in his grandad's pasture with some dynamite that his grandad used for various purposes. This resulted in the stump, along with a considerable amount of dirt, being blown thirty feet across the road.

Amanda was horrified. "You could have been killed!" she exclaimed. "What did your grandad do?"

"He drove down the road shortly after. We hid in the ditch. He stopped his truck, looked at the stump on one side of the road and the hole on the other. He called out the window, 'You boys better get all this debris cleaned up before dinner', and drove on. He never said another word about it."

Amanda laughed irresolutely, wondering how she would cope if her boys pulled such a stunt. Probably not so well. "Your grandfather must be a very unique man."

"He is. You'll like him. I took him to a ghost town when he and Grandmother came to visit me a few years ago. He was walking around the area and noticed an old-fashioned outhouse. He opened the door. There was a dummy dressed like a cowboy sitting inside. Grandad said, 'Excuse me,' closed the door and walked on."

Amanda giggled, "Tell me more."

Rory entertained her with several more childhood adventures. One hot day, his sister, Gloria, her boyfriend, and Rory headed to a lake to swim. On the way, they discussed a horror movie they had seen the night before. Gloria decided to sunbathe on a rubber raft they had brought with them. The guys swam for awhile, ignored by Gloria, lying on her stomach, apparently asleep. Her boyfriend found a plastic mask with a monstrous face in his car, discarded after a party. He put it on, swam under water to the raft and grasped the side, shaking the raft and making unworldly sounds with only his head out of the water. Gloria sat up, shrieked, and (Rory insisted) ran on top of the water to the shore. She was so upset that she broke their date that evening.

Amanda interrupted Rory several times, offering to take the wheel for a spell, but he continued to insist that he wasn't tired. Amanda was amused. "Just like most men. He can't stand riding in the passenger seat," she said to herself.

They stopped for coffee periodically, gas twice, and the miles ticked off on the odometer. About a hundred miles from their destination, they stopped for breakfast. Amanda woke the children, and they grumpily got out and stretched, but brightened by the time orange juice and pancakes appeared in front of them.

Finally, Rory parked the car beside the back door of an attractive house. The lawn was large, with several trees, shrubs, and flowers. A small garden was to the right of the drive, and bird feeders hung from a large tree near the house. There was a detached garage, and farther down the lane, Amanda could see the roof of a barn. A petite, blonde woman and a tall, spare, older man came down the back steps. Rory stepped from the car, hugged the woman and shook hands with the man, as Amanda shepherded the children from the car and stood huddled with them at the edge of the grass.

Rory turned, stepped back to grasp her arm, and led her forward. "Mom, Grandad, this is Amanda," he said. Amanda smiled, struggling to relax, and grasped the hand his mother extended toward her. Rory introduced the children and explained that they were all a little tired and grubby, having driven all night. It was decided that they would rest for an hour, and the children could watch TV if they preferred (they did). Amanda was taken to a lovely room with a breeze coming through an open window. She and Elizabeth would share this room, and the boys would use the sleeping bags Amanda had brought.

Children's voices drifting through the window woke Amanda

from a heavy sleep. She rose languidly from the bed and peeked around the curtain. No one was visible, but she could hear Matthew and Joshua's voices to her left, and remembered there was pasture there. They were probably playing ball. She ran her fingers through her damp hair, then groped under the bed for her shoes. It was hot. The breeze had disappeared. She found the bath down the hall, splashed cool water on her face, and combed her hair. Then she straightened her clothes as best she could and went looking for the others.

The adults were sitting in a downstairs room drinking iced tea. A fan was blowing the air around and it did appear cooler as she descended the three steps to the lower level. Rory rose and greeted her with a smile and led her to the small sofa where he had been sitting. His mother, Dorothy, left to get Amanda a glass of tea.

Grandad greeted her with, "Hey, Yankee Girl, did you have a good nap?"

She answered with a nod and a smile, reassured by his friendliness, and accepted an icy glass of tea from Dorothy.

The conversation continued around her, mostly about people she did not know. Rory held her hand and frequently turned to smile at her. She studied her surroundings, half-listening to their chatter. She had noticed Elizabeth asleep in a big chair in the living room as she walked through. Three bedrooms in an L-shape with a bath in the middle of the long leg, a large living room with a dining nook, a compact kitchen including a small table and three chairs, and this charming garden-like room with south floor-to-ceiling windows. It contained the white wicker sofa she and Rory were sitting on, a matching wicker chair, two massive wooden chairs with plump cushions, and a beautiful glass-top table with a huge ceramic pot holding a trailing green plant that covered most of the table top. The house was spacious, comfortably furnished and apparently built into a slight hill. Amanda started as Rory pressed her fingers and looked at her expectantly. She was vaguely aware that they had been discussing the weekend agenda, and must now have asked what she thought. Her face flushed.

"I'm sorry; I was thinking how charming this room is." She smiled at Dorothy. "The plans you've made are fine. I'm looking forward to meeting everyone," she said, hoping she had not made a fool of herself, and was reassured by Rory's smile.

She helped Dorothy prepare sandwiches for lunch and, after eating, all but Grandad piled into the car to go visiting. On the way back a few hours later, Amanda attempted to sort everyone out whom she had met. An aunt (Dorothy's sister), uncle, Grandad's much younger brother and each of their families, the man Rory had worked for through high school (Amanda was impressed by the obvious respect and friendship they had for each other), and a couple of Rory's childhood friends. At each stop, Amanda had felt that she and the children were being carefully scrutinized.

Even though she had been treated graciously, she had been uneasy, and, she feared, not at her best. She was proud of the way the children had acted and whispered her appreciation to each of them, as she sat in the back seat between Matthew and Joshua with a tired Elizabeth draped in her lap. The children whispered back, asking if they could play outside now.

"I think so, as soon as we get back," their mother answered.

From the afternoon conversations, Amanda gleaned the information she had missed through her earlier inattention. Tomorrow morning to Rory's sister's, a few miles away in another town. Another aunt and uncle would be there. Catfish and hush puppies at the lakeshore tomorrow night, with any or all the relatives who cared to come, would be the highlight marking their visit.

After a delicious dinner of ham, purple-hull peas, homegrown tomatoes, and chocolate cake, the children were allowed to watch an hour of television and Grandad suggested a game of dominoes—42. Amanda had played dominoes with her brothers—child games—but this was a grown-up, serious version. The rules were explained to her and soon she found herself enjoying the game, though not because she was playing well. Grandad promised she would soon be an expert and she laughingly agreed to work at it. They played several hours, fortified with lots of iced tea, and interrupted once while Amanda put the children to bed.

She and Rory stepped into the night while Grandad put the game away and Dorothy rinsed glasses. A soft breeze cooled the air which smelled of pine and an elusive sweetness, possibly honeysuckle. A quarter moon floated in the sky and the stars sparkled, not as brilliant at this lower altitude perhaps, but splendid none-the-less. Silently, they walked up the drive, arm in arm, delighting in the beauty of the night and the sense of being screened from the outside world by the darkness. Rory led Amanda into the shadows of a sweet gum tree and they stood, enfolded in each other's arms, looking at each other, their eyes gleaming in the moonlight. Their kiss was long and as sweet as the air enveloping them.

This is where I belong, Amanda thought. *I'm home. After a tortuous journey, I am home at last.* Reluctantly, she stepped back, shattering the magic, but secure in the knowledge that it would be regained, with increasing sweetness, from this moment on.

"We should go in. Your mom will be wondering what's happened to us."

Rory sighed, "I guess you're right," he said. "You make me very happy, Amanda."

He took her arm and they slowly walked back. Amanda longed to ask what his mother had said about her, if anything, but, at the same time, she feared the answer, so said nothing. Inside, they said good night to each other and went to their beds. Amanda gently moved Elizabeth, who was sprawled across the double bed, to the far side. The breeze whispered through the window, cooling the room. Amanda slept. Some instinct woke her, and she opened her eyes to the sight of Elizabeth sitting Indian-fashion gazing at her. The sun was streaming into the room, and, for a moment, Amanda wondered where she was.

"Mama, I didn't want to wake you, but I have to go to the bathroom," said Elizabeth.

"It's okay, honey. Do you remember where it is? Right down the hall on the left." She looked at her watch, as Elizabeth scrambled over her. Seven-thirty. She hadn't overslept much, then. She heard faint noises filtering through the wall, but could not distinguish them, and jumped out of bed.

After a hearty breakfast, they all piled into the station wagon and drove through narrow, winding roads, guarded on either side by towering pines. It was beautiful, but Amanda felt slightly claustrophobic at such a restricted view.

Soon they stopped in front of Gloria's house. Some sort of commotion—shouts and an angry voice—could be heard coming from some outbuildings several hundred yards away. After greeting his sister and introducing Amanda and the children, Rory asked what was going on out there.

"Don't bring it up in front of Bill," Gloria advised. "He had trouble with the bull this morning. It got out and ran into the dog kennel. Bill can't get it out because there is no room for it to turn around. He is so angry he is nailing the entrance shut. He said the bull could stay there until it starved!"

Rory laughed and said he would go and see if he could help.

Gloria told the children they could watch TV and introduced them to her four-year-old daughter, Jennifer, who smiled shyly from behind her mother's legs. She was soon coaxed to lead the way to the family room and Elizabeth took her hand as Matthew and Joshua followed.

"She's darling," said Amanda, as she accepted the proffered apron. Gloria smiled and asked if she would make the salad. Amanda studied Gloria as they worked. She knew Gloria was a few years older than Rory. She had the same coloring as her brother, and was taller than Amanda. She wore blue shorts, a pull-over knit shirt, and sandals, and had an infectious grin. Amanda liked her immediately, and they were soon chattering away with Dorothy joining in. Amanda didn't mind answering the friendly questions about herself and the children, and she asked questions, too. She learned that Gloria was a secretary for an executive in a plant a few miles away, and that she and Bill were planning to build a new house.

Dorothy's youngest sister, with husband and three daughters, ages about ten to fourteen, arrived, bringing them to a small crowd of about fifteen. A smiling Bill was introduced to Amanda, the morning's trouble apparently forgotten or resolved.

It was a pleasant day. The hamburgers were devoured with relish, as was the pecan pie. The children played with few complaints, and only minor scratches. It was late afternoon when they headed home, a little sunburned, and a bit tired, but with the promise to meet at the lake later.

They bathed and donned fresh clothes and in no time were back in the car. About half-way to their destination, the car gave a lurch and the engine stopped. Rory fought the wheel to guide it off the pavement. He and Grandad checked all they knew that could be wrong to no avail. The engine would not turn over.

Rory walked to find a telephone, and the rest of them sat or walked along the verge. The sun waned and the first star appeared before Rory returned with Bill. They went through the check procedure again, with the same results—nothing. Bill took them back to Grandad's, then he and Rory returned to tow the car to a garage in the next town. Of course, it was closed on a Sunday evening, but Bill knew the owner and thought he would look it over on Monday morning, despite it being a holiday. That was all that could be done at present. Bill and Rory returned about eight, hot, dusty, tired, and

Rory, at least, was disgusted. His normal good humor returned somewhat after another bath and some food.

They were to have started home the next morning, and discussed what they might do, realizing they would have to wait for the diagnosis of the car before definite plans could be made. They finally decided to get a good night's sleep and tackle the problem in the morning.

Amanda could not sleep. She willed her body to lie still, so as not to wake Elizabeth. The night was hot, Amanda's legs cramped from sitting all day, and her sunburned arms stung. This, combined with concern about how they would get home, made sleep elusive. After half an hour she could lie there no longer, and slipped out of bed to sit on the floor by the window. The curtain fell limply to the sill—no breeze tonight. Her thoughts swirled in circles—the logistics of getting home, never by Tuesday morning, of course. She had requested a half-day from work on Tuesday, to register the children in school. The personal—did Dorothy approve of Amanda? After all, Rory was her only son, and the baby of the family. She had been very kind. Grandad was a sweetheart, and appeared to like her. Gloria was friendly, but Amanda had felt her appraising eyes. The aunts? Amanda couldn't tell.

"Well, I was myself, and I did the best I could," she whispered to the night. Her mind sorted through the various conversations for clues as to how she stood, but she came to no conclusion. The children had behaved very well. Matthew and Joshua had almost got into a fight, Joshua had argued with one of the girls about whose turn it was in a game (Amanda suspected this was his way of showing that he liked the little girl), and Elizabeth had pouted when she didn't get her way once—all minor, surely, for children during most of a day at play with strangers. She went over it all—again and again.

She prayed for peace in her heart, but it was as though her message wouldn't go through. She had experienced this before at times, and knew it to be temporary. Her thoughts were too chaotic and unfocused. Jesus was there, but she was disconnected. After what seemed like hours, she vaguely realized she had nodded off once or twice and slowly got to her feet and laid down on the bed on her stomach, her arms cradled under her head. The next thing she knew, it was daylight and the birds were singing outside the window.

Later, she felt that the minutes after waking were perhaps the best part of that day. The children were the least trouble. Largely left to their own devices, they explored the stream, the woods, and whatever else Amanda prudently didn't ask about. She had voiced a fear of snakes, but after being told by Rory, Dorothy, and Grandad, not to worry, as snakes are afraid of people and will run away, she kept quiet, although she was not wholly convinced.

By evening, after Rory spent hours at the garage and made several phone calls, he learned that the car would need extensive repairs—more than its worth warranted. If Rory chose to have it repaired, it would take at least a week. He was agitated and apologetic, even though Amanda continued to assure him that the breakdown was unforeseen and no one's fault. Still, she had no answer to their dilemma. How were they to get home?

They rehashed the problem between periods of silence. Finally, after listening to them for some time, Grandad took matters into his own hands. They would take his car. Dorothy would drive. She could take her time returning, and visit her brother and his family on the way home. Feeble protests were ignored and it was settled. They would leave early the next morning. Bill would sell the car for what he could get. Exhausted and relieved, everyone went to bed.

The trip was difficult. Amanda and the children were cramped in the backseat, and Rory fidgeted in the passenger seat, while Dorothy concentrated on her driving. They went as swiftly as possible, stopping for gas and sandwiches when necessary. Amanda tried to keep the children occupied with word games and stories, but they were sulky and uncooperative. The road seemed endless. Amanda wearily dropped her head back against the seat. Tears threatened. Rory had planned this trip carefully, hoping she and his family would forge a positive relationship. It had started well, but ended disastrously, all the same.

Please, Jesus, just let us get home safely and as soon as possible. It was a sweltering day. The windows were lowered and the hot wind blew through the car with a constant whistle. But even bad days end, and this one was no exception. It was almost midnight when the car stopped at Amanda's house. She tugged sleepy children from the back and searched for her key. Luggage could wait for tomorrow. Rory took her key, opened the door, and gently prodded the children inside. He kissed Amanda briefly, told her he would see her the next day, and ordered her to get some sleep. She smiled weakly and locked the door behind him. The children were sitting in a row on the couch, seemingly not knowing where they were or what to do. She gently ushered them to their rooms, helped them strip to their underwear, and kissed them good night.

In her bedroom, Amanda stared, woodenly, at her bed. *Be it ever so humble, there's no place like home*, flitted through her mind and she uttered a tired laugh. She was asleep as soon as her head hit the pillow.

15

I will fear no evil

(Psalm 23:4)

Laughter and unidentifiable sounds wakened her. She glanced at her bedside clock—7:30! She jumped out of bed. All three children were in the boys' room and dressed. They were pulling toys from the chest with delight, as though greeting old friends they had thought never to see again. Elizabeth was sitting in the middle of the bed, and Amanda sensed that she had been bouncing there with abandon.

"What's going on guys?" she asked.

They turned to stone at her voice and stared at her with wide round eyes.

She smiled. "Better clean up the mess while I fix breakfast," she said and continued down the hall.

She called her office while the children ate their cereal and explained what had happened, promising to come in after lunch—no problem there. The children would be in two different schools, and she managed to arrange a visit to each for registration. She then called Debbie to explain why she had not brought the children over the day before, and promised to give her all the details later.

After a quick breakfast, the children were sent to dress for the school visits, and Amanda sat for a minute to catch her breath and finish her coffee, now cold and bitter. Rory opened the door after a quick knock, and entered laden with various bags and other traveling paraphernalia, which he dropped on the living room floor. He ran his fingers through his hair and looked at Amanda.

"Are you speaking to me today?" he asked, not smiling.

Amanda went to him, put her arms around him, and lifted her face to kiss him on the cheek. "Come, have some coffee," she said and drew him into the kitchen.

He sat down and sighed. "I don't know how to begin to tell you how sorry I am," he said.

She placed a steaming mug in front of him and kissed the top of his head. "The trip back yesterday was rather grim, yes. All your fault? No! Sweetheart, don't apologize. If this is the worst that happens to us …" she smiled, "I *was* looking forward to catfish and hush puppies, though. So next time …!"

Rory returned her smile. "You're not angry? I thought…."

She leaned over and stopped him with a kiss. He grasped her arms and returned the kiss, hungrily. She pulled away and poured more coffee.

"What will you do about a car?" she asked.

"I'll try to buy another one today. I had planned to trade that old one in after Christmas anyway. I don't have a trade-in now, but I should be able to make some kind of deal."

"Of course you will." After a moment she asked, "How is your mother?"

Rory glanced at his watch, "She wants to leave about ten. I have to get back."

"I'm registering the kids for school this morning. We have an appointment at 9:30, so I have to get going, too."

She followed him to the door, and he took her in his arms. "I love you so much. You're the best thing that ever happened to me." He paused, "I was afraid you might throw me out."

"I love you, too, and I thought you might think I was a jinx and never come back."

They laughed, and he said he would see her later.

Registration was relatively painless. Amanda had all necessary records and documentation. She dropped the children off at Debbie's after a quick lunch and went to work.

She sensed trouble as she walked into her office. Her boss was leaning in the doorway to his office. He leered at her and mumbled something about her not earning a half-day off. She settled at her desk with apprehension. Later, he called her in, ostensibly to check on some correspondence. He dictated a couple of short letters, such that Amanda had been routinely handling on her own, and then invited her to meet him after work at a bar down the street, saying that she owed him a half-day's work, that she must be very lonely, that he could take care of that, and there would be no docking of her pay.

Amanda told him bluntly and heatedly that she was not interested, and that she thought they had settled this earlier. She ended by telling him she was engaged.

"I don't see a ring," he sneered.

"Nevertheless, it's true. Now leave me alone!" and she stormed back to her office.

She stopped beside her desk, seething with anger, breathing hard, her hands clenched. It took several minutes for her to gain control. When she was calmer, she covered her typewriter, grabbed her purse, told the receptionist she had to leave and ran to her car. She sat there, gripping the wheel for some time, afraid to drive, determined not to cry. Finally, she started the car and, as she drove, she spoke aloud to her Friend, pouring out her anguish. "I know vengeance is to be left to you, Lord, but right now, I could cheerfully rip out his fingernails, his eyes, and a few other things!" After a few minutes of this, she ran down, and was appalled at the violence in her heart and her voice, and asked God to forgive her. The outburst had a cathartic effect, purging her of deep anger, and by the time she reached Debbie's, she had managed to put the entire incident to the back of her mind.

She spent an hour there, healing as she was drawn into the innocent atmosphere. All five children wanted to tell about their afternoon and it was some time before she could tell Debbie about the trip. Debbie listened with sympathy. Suddenly a smile appeared on Debbie's face, grew wider, and Debbie exploded in laughter.

Amanda stared at her, perplexed, a frown on her face.

"I'm sorry, Amanda. It just struck me how funny it is. You, all prim and proper, wanting to make a good impression on your in-laws-to-be, and Rory wanting to show you off, and having planned so carefully, then ..." she giggled, "then, his mother has to bring you home!"

"You have a strange sense of humor, Debbie," Amanda said not smiling, "It was not amusing, sitting in that hot car with three kids all day, packed in the back like sardines."

Debbie sobered at once. "Of course it wasn't. That must have been dreadful." She paused. "But the situation, as a whole—like a soap opera or something."

Amanda was thoughtful. A glimmer of a smile touched her face. She looked at Debbie, who was watching her hopefully, "I'm beginning to see what you mean, I think—best laid plans, and all that. Then everything goes wrong."

"Yes! Like when the bride falls as she walks down the aisle. That sort of thing!" Debbie's voice pleaded for Amanda to concur.

"I think you have been listening to David and Rory too much lately. I might expect this type of thing from them, but I'm honestly surprised to hear it from you," she said reproachfully.

Debbie's face fell, and Amanda relented and patted her hand.

"It's okay. In a week I'll be able to appreciate the humor of it … maybe," she conceded.

"You aren't angry, are you?" asked Debbie.

"No, not angry. Surprised, as I said, that you looked at the situation from a totally different perspective. I'm glad you did, actually. I need to 'lighten up' as the kids say. Well, I have to go. I wonder what the kids are doing? They're awfully quiet."

The children were watching television, and not in a hurry to go home, but Amanda banded them together and into the car. At home, she sorted through the boys' closet and chest of drawers, locating clothes suitable for school. They had outgrown many items over the summer. The child-support check was due this week, and she planned to go shopping on Saturday. She made a list as she worked. Shoes—a must, two pairs of pants each, three shirts each if she could afford them, socks—definitely, underwear could wait.

Then Elizabeth's turn. Amanda didn't know what little girls wore to school here and decided to call Debbie for help. Mostly pants and blouses, she was told, sweaters later, some dresses and skirts, sneakers for the most part. She had always sewn most of Elizabeth's clothes, and several dresses still fit, although they were a little bit short. She could get by with two new pairs of pants for now. Blouses—no problem, socks and sneakers needed.

Amanda sighed. She hated shopping, and was wont to put it off as long as possible. Procrastination would not serve this time, and she vowed to get it over with early Saturday and be done with it.

No doubt, tomorrow the children would bring home sheets filled with lists of supplies which they would need by the next day. She had gone through this drill before, and was resigned.

Deliberately turning her thoughts to more pleasant tasks, she prepared dinner and supervised baths. She allowed the children to watch a half-hour of television, and she checked her budget while keeping an eye on the programming.

Rory arrived about nine o'clock, as she was putting the children to bed, and helped tuck them in and hear their prayers. She heard his intake of breath when his name was mentioned at the end.

Amanda poured fresh coffee, and Rory settled on the couch. She wanted to hear what his family, especially his mother, had said about her, yet she fiddled with the coffee tray, straightened pillows, picked up a book and placed it on the shelf, delaying the moment of truth.

Rory snatched her hand as she walked by the third or fourth time. "Sit down, Honey! You're making me dizzy." He coaxed her to sit beside him. "What are you so jittery about?" he asked.

"Maybe a change in the weather or something," she answered evasively. "Did you buy a car?'

"I thought you'd never ask! Come out and see it! It's sporty, and cost more than I planned. It was all I could find on short notice."

He drew her outside. A sleek, metallic green with black vinyl top sports coupe was parked behind her drab Ford compact.

"Oh! My goodness!" Amanda gasped.

Rory grinned. "Pretty sporty isn't it? See the chrome wheels?" He went to the driver's side and unlocked the hood. "Look at this engine—lots of horsepower."

Amanda looked. She was not mechanically minded, but she could recognize most of the parts under the hood of her little stick-shift car and, in general, knew their purpose. She had never seen the likes of this. The entire space was filled with the huge engine, hoses ran from here to there connecting—she had no idea what. It was impressive, to say the least.

"Oh, my goodness." she repeated, dumbfounded.

Rory gently closed the hood, walked to the passenger side and opened the door. The back seat is rather small, but I think the kids will fit, don't you?" he asked. "Get in and see how you like it," he urged.

"It's very nice, Rory," Amanda said, as she slid into the bucket seat. "Beautiful upholstery," she remarked, rubbing her hand along the shiny black leather.

"It has a tape deck, too—even a few tapes were left in the pocket."

Amanda smiled, thinking he was like a little boy with a new toy, (an old cliche, but so apt). "It's beautiful! I like it."

Rory gave her a grateful smile. "Would you like to drive it around the block?"

"Oh, no! I wouldn't know how.... I mean, I hate driving a new car. It takes me awhile to get used to it and this one.... I wouldn't dare touch it."

Rory laughed. "It's easy, all automatic. We'll take it out Sunday where there's not much traffic."

He continued to enthuse about the car for several more minutes. Then they went back inside and Amanda poured more coffee.

The car was nice, actually beautiful (no other adjectives came to her), and she enjoyed seeing the pleasure on Rory's face. She wanted to share his excitement and did her best to ask intelligent questions and reply to his questions with equal enthusiasm. It just wasn't in her. She appreciated a car, cared if the color was pleasing, and the shape. Beyond that, a vehicle was simply a means of taking her where she wanted to go and carrying what she wanted to take somewhere else.

After a while, it had all been said, and Rory took a sip of his lukewarm coffee.

Amanda took the opportunity to ask if his Mom got off all right. She had—shortly after ten. He didn't elaborate and Amanda wondered if she was going to be forced to bring up the subject that was uppermost in her thoughts. Disliking dissembling, she came to the point.

"Did your mother say anything about me? And the kids?" she asked.

Rory's surprised look confirmed that he hadn't given it a

thought. "Well, she liked you, of course," he said and turned back to the stack of records he was examining.

Amanda waited. She realized this was going to be more difficult than she had imagined. Rory selected a record, placed it on the machine and sat beside Amanda, his head back, eyes closed, feet on the table—perfectly at ease.

Amanda frowned, and murmured: "I don't want to extract information like a dentist pulling teeth! Another cliche! I'm brilliant tonight!"

"Gloria said she didn't think I had such good taste," Rory said, not opening his eyes. "Mom said you weren't what she had expected," he added, a full minute later.

Amanda sat quietly, smiling. *I'm going to get it in installments!* she thought.

"Everyone said the kids were very well behaved."

The piano music emanating from the stereo was soothing. *Don't go to sleep*, Amanda pleaded, silently.

Aloud she asked, "Would you like more coffee?" (She winced as she heard herself. Her scintillating conversation tonight would put anyone to sleep, but her mind was filled with getting answers, and not with being interesting and entertaining.)

"What? Oh, sorry, I guess I'm about to give out," Rory answered. "No more coffee." He shifted to a straighter position, taking his feet off the table, and looking at her. "I thought we might go look at rings this weekend. What do you think?"

At the word *ring*, Amanda's thoughts retrieved, from the deep recess in her mind, the incident at work. "I don't see a ring!" she said in a strange voice. Her face clouded, her eyes stared at nothing.

"What are you talking about?" Rory demanded, "What ring?"

Amanda gasped, not realizing she had spoken aloud. "It's nothing, something that someone said. Forget I mentioned it." Her voice belied her words and soon Rory had the full story.

"I'll have a talk with this guy in the morning!" Rory said, gritting his teeth. A fierce look distorted his handsome features.

"No!" she exclaimed. "You mustn't. I can handle him. I've done it before."

"It's happened before?" Rory had never raised his voice in Amanda's hearing before, and she was a little frightened by his intensity.

"Rory, I've had to deal with men like him several times where I worked," she said in a small voice. "It's not that unusual, although it is a part of working that I hate." Her voice broke. "But I will take care of it, believe me. I didn't intend you to know." She spoke with more spirit. "Please, don't do anything. I'm hoping a civil service job will open up soon. I did well on the test, and was told I should hear from them in a few months."

Rory was not appeased, and they argued for several minutes. At last, Rory relaxed somewhat. But he made Amanda promise to tell him it if occurred again.

Then, after a few minutes, he brought up the subject of rings again.

Amanda sighed. Another difficult subject. She had been thinking about rings for days, and she was afraid Rory would not agree with her wishes. At least, it would probably not be easy to convince him. She prayed for the right words as she took both his hands in hers and looked into his eyes.

"Please listen to what I have to say before *you* say anything." She paused and Rory nodded. "I love you very much, more than I thought possible. I didn't know love could be like what we are building, and I want to be your wife more than anything in the world." Again she paused and took a deep breath. "I don't want an engagement ring."

Rory opened his mouth, and she placed her fingers over it, to stop the words.

"Ssh, please let me tell you why," she pleaded. "I want a wide gold wedding band, one that clearly shows a never-ending circle, no end to our marriage, no weak place where it can be broken, nothing sharp or pointed to take away from its clear and simple symbol of eternal love." Her eyes pleaded for understanding.

Rory looked at her in bewilderment. They sat, looking at each other, not moving, for several moments, as though sending and receiving messages with their eyes. The only sound was the music.

Rory spoke first. "I understand what you're telling me. 'A clear symbol of eternal love'—it's a beautiful way to say it." He stopped and continued to search her face. "We'll get the rings you want. That's what I want, too." He smiled at her.

Apprehension fled from Amanda's face. She smiled. "Thank you so much for understanding," she said in a choked voice.

"You know I can't deny you anything, even if I wanted to. And in this case, I don't want to. I hadn't thought about it, just assumed you would want an engagement ring, but … well, what you said, I agree with it."

"You don't mind then?"

"I just want to make you happy. The only thing about an engagement ring is, it shows everyone you're promised to me—you know—'Hands off!', 'No trespassing!'—that sort of thing." He grinned at her and gave her a hug.

Amanda returned the hug with enthusiasm. "I promise you that everyone will know—they will know by looking at me, and if they don't, I'll tell them," she said, in a voice muffled by his shirt collar.

They held each other, their hearts and spirits blending, building a foundation of trust and faith in each other. Then Rory rose, lifting her to stand beside him, and kissed her good night. There was no need for words.

Amanda walked into her office the next morning, braced for any eventuality.

"The boss has taken the rest of the week off. He's gone to Las Vegas," the receptionist told her.

Amanda had wondered if the receptionist had been accosted on the job, but she didn't feel she knew her well enough to ask, even though they got along well. Now, she caught a look of relief mixed with satisfaction on the young girl's face, and decided she had probably gone through the same ordeal. Her face hardened. *Someone should string that guy up!* she thought. The loathing that boiled up inside her, made her slightly sick, and she realized that she did not know herself as well as she had thought. It was sobering to acknowledge that such venom was within her, and she resolved to never let her temper get out of control.

16

Delight thyself also in the Lord; and he shall give thee the desires of thine heart

(Psalm 37:4)

Rory came in while Amanda and the children were eating supper. She had decided he was not able to come by for some reason this evening.

"Sorry I'm late," he said, and laid a pile of books on the floor by the door. "I had to stand in line for hours to get books and fill out all the Veteran's forms."

"What are you taking?" asked Amanda as she set his plate and silver on the table.

"Algebra and Trig, and American History," replied Rory, as he sat down. "You can look at the books."

Amanda took her plate to the kitchen, wiped the table where she had eaten, and placed the stack of books there. She read the titles and flipped through the books. There were several for the history class. "Lots of reading and math work. You must take enough time to study. Do you think you could study here part of the time?"

"No way! You're too much a distraction." He grinned at her and Matthew snickered.

"All right," Amanda said and smiled. "But you take all the time you need to study—at your house. Just tell me you need to study, okay?"

"No problem. I'll start reading them in the morning."

"In the morning? But classes don't start until next week."

"I know. I always read the books before classes start. It helps a lot—I'm always a little ahead that way."

Amanda stared at him. "That's incredible! Actually, it's a very smart thing to do!"

"Seemed that way to me," he said and shrugged. "Is there any more spaghetti? I'm starved."

Amanda took his plate to the kitchen for a refill.

A few days later, she was checking the newspaper ads for Saturday's food specials. She was having trouble completing her grocery list. She realized her eating habits had been erratic, to say the least, all summer. Now that the children were home, regular, nutritious meals were required. She had always enjoyed cooking—that was not the problem. She had made a budget, and, while she must shop carefully, money was not the problem either. It finally dawned on her—the problem was that she knew very little about Rory's food preferences. He would probably have dinner at her house at least twice a week, and she didn't know what he would like. They had fixed sandwiches, soup, and omelets during the summer, but little else. They had eaten out quite a lot and Rory usually ordered steak or shrimp, and he had enjoyed eating at Mexican restaurants. *And don't forget,* she reminded herself, *he likes fish and rice and gravy. I can afford that,* she thought, *but I refuse to color it green!* And vegetables—she had never noticed him eating them except potatoes and salad. She liked vegetables—all vegetables, and had served a variety to the children so they would learn to like them, too. This had proven successful to a point. Her rule was that you must try new things at least three times, and if it is not a favorite, you, thereafter, must have a small serving whenever it is on the menu. "So we'll see what happens," she said to herself and added several different vegetables, both fresh and frozen, to her list.

She found out what happens two days later when Rory was at the house for dinner. She had prepared oven-fried chicken, buttered rice, broccoli with cheese sauce, and a tossed salad.

After the blessing, bowls of food were passed around. Rory looked at the bowl that Elizabeth handed to him.

"We're having seaweed for dinner?" he asked.

Amanda looked at Matthew and Joshua. It was not one of their favorites, either, although Elizabeth liked it. The boys were looking at Rory with awe, wondering what their mother would do and say. Amanda wondered, too. She felt she was on her own with this one.

"Yes, it's seaweed broccoli and *everyone* (she gave Rory a meaningful glance) must try the new cheese sauce." She gave the boys a no nonsense now look, and saw that Rory noticed.

Comprehension dawned on his face, and he said: "Hmm, the cheese sauce looks good." He took a small serving and smiled at Amanda.

She took it as an apology, and smiled a thank you back at him.

Over the next few months, she learned that he liked corn, peas, and beans—canned, frozen, fresh, or dried—spinach, turnip greens, and salads. Fresh tomatoes were especially favored. Broccoli and cauliflower, he would tolerate, if smothered with cheese. He absolutely refused to consider liver, sauerkraut, or beets, and Amanda served those only when she knew he would not appear for dinner.

One Saturday morning in late September, Rory and the children arranged for Amanda to visit Debbie. They were going to "make a surprise." She was not to return before two in the afternoon. Amanda acquiesced gracefully. Her birthday was the following week, and she assumed the surprise concerned this, although she had no idea what they were up to.

She returned, at the appointed time, with David, Debbie, and the girls, and was presented with a cake decorated with fresh flowers and a slightly wobbly message: *Happy Birthday Mama*, in pink frosting. They had a wonderful party. After eating cake and pistachio ice cream (Amanda's favorite), Elizabeth proudly handed her a package with a homemade card attached depicting a mommy, two little boys, and one little girl. It was signed: Love from Matthew, Joshua, and Elizabeth. They watched intently as she unwrapped the package—a box of dusting powder. Amanda's eyes were moist as she hugged each child. She looked at Rory, hoping to convey her thought: *You're a very special man.* Anne and Sarah handed her a wrapped box which turned out to be stationery with a lovely mountain scene in one corner, with pine scent. She hugged them, too. Rory told her his gift would come later—he was taking her out to dinner.

After everyone left (Rory would change and be back in about an hour), the children enthusiastically told her about their morning. They were amazed that Rory could bake a cake so easily, and he had let each one have a turn with the mixer. Amanda was a little amazed herself. Rory could, and willingly did any chore in the house—laundry, ironing, vacuuming—and he could cook, too! What a handy person to have around.

She had decided to leave Matthew in charge this evening. All three were adamant that they no longer needed a sitter, and they promised to obey the rules. They were not to leave the house. They were to let no one in the house. They were not to tell anyone on the phone that they were alone. These, together with general rules of no fighting, no watching unsuitable TV, etc., were reviewed. Amanda posted the name and phone number of the restaurant on the refrigerator door. Then she went to bathe, promising to use her new powder.

Rory took her to a Polynesian restaurant, which was rapidly becoming a favored place. They began with a glass of wine, and as they sipped, Amanda thanked Rory for spending the time with the children, and told him how much they enjoyed it.

"The cake was delicious. You'll make some girl a great husband!"

"It was fun, and yes, I plan to!" he said, joining in her festive mood.

The dinner was sumptuous. They chose a combination plate with a variety of house specialties, and dallied over the meal, enjoying the food and the atmosphere.

When they were seated in the car, afterwards, Rory reached behind the car seat and handed Amanda a large box wrapped in silver ribbon. She gasped when she saw the store name—the most expensive women's shop in town, she had heard.

"Wait until we get to your house to open it," he said.

As soon as they were inside, Amanda opened the box. Inside were two pairs of slacks—one solid blue and one blue plaid. They were beautifully made, of rich materials.

"They're lovely," breathed Amanda, running the fabric through her fingers, "but it's too much!"

"There were some other things I wanted to get for you. They can wait until next time. I had never been in a store like that before. I described you and they told me to sit in a chair in this almost empty room. A minute or so later, a model came in wearing those blue pants. She walked, and turned around once or twice and left. Then another model came in with the other pants on and did the same thing. I couldn't decide which ones I liked best, so I took both of them. I hope they fit?"

Amanda checked the tags. They were her size. "Rory they're perfect, but you shouldn't be so extravagant, I...." She saw the beginning of a frown on his face, and his lips began to purse, and she hastily revised what she had been about to say.

"And I love them. Thank you." She watched Rory's face change as he smiled. "Thank you for the beautiful slacks, for the scrumptious dinner, and all the rest of the day that you planned."

Rory took her in his arms, "Happy Birthday, Amanda."

Amanda's heart thumped at the look in his eyes. *The greatest gift he has given me is himself,* she thought, *I want to see him look at me just this way every day for the rest of my life.*

Their embrace and kisses were sweet, and, too soon, Rory went home. But the sweetness lingered with Amanda through her bedtime ritual, through her prayers, and into her dreams.

The weeks that followed were a time of discovery and communion for all five of them. Autumn was Amanda's favorite time of year, and in October they drove into the mountains to see the aspens that had turned into golden fire. It was spectacular—as though a careless artist had sloshed paint from his huge bucket, nearly covering the mountainsides. Amanda had never seen such beauty. She gazed and gazed, enthralled, and almost oblivious of the others, taking the sight into her soul, until the sun disappeared and they turned back. Her camera lay at her feet, forgotten until dusk had rendered it useless. This was regrettable, but she knew that nothing could erase the pictures from her memory.

They played outdoor games in the park during Indian Summer, and board games in the kitchen on cool Saturday afternoons. Rory liked shopping and frequently took the children when they needed supplies or common items of clothing, relieving Amanda of a hated chore.

On the evenings Rory had classes, he would sometimes drop by Amanda's for a few minutes to relax. When Amanda had asked him when he studied, he had said early mornings. She had been skeptical and was delighted when he showed her his first quarter grades—very respectable. The children did well in school the first six weeks, too—A's and B's. They had made friends and there were frequently other children in the house after supper and on weekends. The boys went bicycling, when the streets were dry. Joshua got a warning from a policeman for going too fast down a hill. Elizabeth was learning how much fun a telephone could be.

The children were accepting Rory as part of their family, no longer treating him as company. Slowly, he was being woven into the pattern of their daily lives. Elizabeth had endorsed Rory's almost daily visits within a week or so. One evening she brought the book Amanda had been reading aloud to the children, and asked Rory to read. He did so, with Elizabeth sitting next to him. Joshua appropriated several of Rory's jokes and riddles and practiced telling them to his siblings until they groaned in protest. Matthew, naturally more reserved, warmed gradually. Rory had offered to help him with math, and he was impressed when Rory taught him shortcuts and tricks with numbers. Rory also taught the boys the rudiments of chess, and they played with great enthusiasm, though with a little less skill.

Amanda was getting more accustomed to Rory's jokes, but he still *caught* her, more often than not. One evening he was sitting on the couch, while she went to the kitchen for coffee.

"I heard a little joke, today," he called to her.

She stuck her head around the doorway. "Oh, what was it?"

"It was so little, it didn't matter any more," he said in an offhand manner.

She stared at him for a few seconds, then, "Oh, you!," she exclaimed, and threw a dishtowel, missing him by a yard.

He laughed and tossed the towel back, then sat with his feet on the coffee table. Amanda sighed and smiled as she tossed the towel into the laundry basket and picked up the coffee mugs.

Rory was generous with gifts, and not only on birthdays. If Amanda, or the children, expressed a desire for something, it often showed up in a day or two with "I saw this and I knew you would like it," or "Is this what you've been wanting?" Rory would say and hand it to her or one of the children. Amanda tried to put a damper on this practice, without much success so far as the children were concerned, but she learned to keep her own mouth closed within Rory's hearing. Still, Rory brought little gifts that she treasured, and that made her love him more than expensive gifts ever could.

Late evenings, Rory and Amanda would talk or listen to music, sometimes dancing in the small living room. They went out to dinner perhaps once a week, and, rarely, to a movie. They often chaffed at the reality of the long months until April. At those times, Rory would abruptly kiss her on the cheek and retreat, leaving Amanda tense and sleepless and unable to pray. In the morning, she would feel remorse and ask God to forgive her rebellion, and thank Him for covering them with His strength. Joy and peace would return to her heart.

Rory's birthday was in mid-November and Joshua's was about a week later. They planned separate celebrations.

Rory's favorite cake was German chocolate. Amanda made one with four layers. Dinner was fried chicken. Chocolate ice cream went with the cake. The children decorated the living room and dining area with balloons and candles. Their gift was shaving lotion, a new scent Amanda thought Rory had not used. Amanda gave him a brief-case, and a felt hat he had admired. Rory splashed a bit of lotion on his face at once so the children could pass judgment. They laughed and sniffed, creating a contest amongst themselves until Amanda laughingly called a halt to their game.

After the children were in bed, they sat in their usual places on the couch.

"I've never had a birthday party before, that I can remember, anyway," Rory admitted, "you have no idea what this evening has meant to me."

Amanda squeezed his hand and told him that he would have one every year until he got tired of them.

Rory went to the stereo and spent several moments choosing an album. As the slow jazz music began, he pulled Amanda to her feet, and they danced, holding each other closely. The little room was infused with warmth.

The next weekend, Amanda made another chocolate cake—this one in the shape of a ship. Joshua invited three friends to the party.

The afternoon was filled with noisy games. Then Amanda brought in the cake, frosted in red, white, and blue, with tiny paper flags waving—all lit by eleven candles. The cake and strawberry ice cream quickly disappeared. The party ended with Joshua opening gifts, including a clock radio from Amanda and Rory.

17

Unto thee, O God, do we give thanks

(Psalm 75:1)

Amanda invited her entire family for Thanksgiving, and they came, bringing their favorite delicacies to add to the turkey and corn bread dressing Amanda provided. Even Lynn, her second sister, came from Texas, with her husband Will, and her little boy. Rory had now met each of Amanda's siblings. The little house almost exploded with laughter and fun. They played games, related family member escapades, watched college arch-rivals play football on television, rooting for their favorites and participating in friendly arguments. It was a beautiful Indian summer day, and the fun spilled into the backyard. Rory took on the role of host, even carving the turkey, and took candid photos of everyone.

In the evening, they snacked on left-overs, and her sisters and brother, who lived hours away began the long trip home, taking her two younger sisters with them. Amanda's parents would stay overnight.

The children began to run down, the remaining adults sprawled on couch and chairs in the living room, with just enough light conversation to keep them awake. Soon David and Debbie left with Anne and Sarah, and Rory followed shortly after. Amanda sent her children to bed and prepared her bedroom for her parents. She took her night things to the bathroom. She would sleep on the couch. She had been bursting with happiness all day. It had been years since she had celebrated Thanksgiving with her family, and she had never been the hostess for such a large gathering. Now, as she pulled a blanket under her chin, joy permeated every cell of her body. It had been a glorious day. Her family and Rory had made it perfect. Rory had been superb—helping in the kitchen, supervising the children, joining in the conversations, making jokes. He was blending in with her obstreperous family like a flower in a spring bouquet. She was so joyful that little chuckles gushed, unbidden, from her smiling mouth. She stifled them with her hand and buried her head under the covers, so as not to wake anyone. This joy metamorphosed into a prayer of praise and thanksgiving for the flawless day.

An eight-inch snowfall the next week inspired Rory to help the children build a snow fort in the backyard. It collapsed a couple of times, but they persisted and ended with a warm cavern about two feet by four with a wind-screening wall in front. They came inside at lunchtime, half-frozen and laughing, and bringing clumps of snow with them, which plopped to the floor as they removed their wet clothing. Amanda cheerfully swept the snow clumps out the door, and mopped up the melted mess. She dished up hot dogs and chili, and they were soon warm inside and out.

As they began to eat, she shoved icy clothes into the washer, giving it a sympathetic pat as she turned the knob to the short wash cycle. Dripping boots were placed near furnace vents on several layers of newspaper. This routine would be repeated later in the afternoon. Amanda hoped the washer, dryer, and the clothing would outlast the winter.

18

Give, and it shall be given unto you

(Luke 6:38)

Rory and Amanda shopped together for the children's Christmas gifts. Her budget was limited and she chose carefully, balancing just-for-fun items with the practical. Rory was enjoying himself by following behind her and placing toys she had put back on the shelf into his own basket. She remonstrated, saying he would spoil them, and, she added: "Christmas is giving, but mostly it should celebrate the birth of Christ. It's His birthday!"

"We'll do both," Rory promised, as he picked up another toy. Amanda shook her head and smiled at him.

Christmas cards were addressed, most with accompanying letters, to old friends and Amanda's family. Rory's Mom, Grandad, and sister Gloria, were added to Amanda's list and she spent many minutes formulating the proper messages. She took the children shopping for gifts to exchange with each other, and a gift they would send to their dad. Her family had drawn names at Thanksgiving, and she bought and wrapped those. Christmas Day would be spent with her family. They planned to leave early Christmas morning, stay overnight, and return the day after.

The second week in December, Rory brought a beautiful pine tree, about six feet tall, just right for placing in front of the picture window. Amanda collected the boxes of trimmings from the basement and they decorated the tree with lights and ornaments, many of which Amanda had made over the years. Later, they sat on the floor admiring their handiwork, munching popcorn and sipping from mugs of cocoa with silky marshmallows floating on top.

One night, they drove around the city looking at lights and decorations on homes, and downtown to the Holly Sugar Building. Each year, the huge display windows in the front of the building facing the street were filled with magic. Lights, pretend snow, bells and ornaments, candy canes, Santas and reindeer, and stuffed bears and other animals dressed in festive costumes, all combined to create a wonderland. The children looked for a half hour or more, running from window to window as toys moved in their planned automated patterns and Christmas music pealed forth from loud speakers. Rory and Amanda were as enchanted as the children.

They attended Elizabeth's Christmas program at school where she sang with the choir and recited a poem. Matthew and Joshua had a similar program, respectively portraying a shepherd and a sheep in a tableaux. Amanda wiped a few tears as she watched. Her babies were growing up. Their church presented a play and concert, and the children sang in the children's choir. Matthew and Joshua sang with gusto, but Elizabeth was developing a strong interest in group singing and a delight in performing. She worked very hard to perfect her voice.

Rory's company gave a Christmas Dance for their employees. Amanda had no evening dress, although she did have a pair of silver evening slippers. With only a week's notice, she had frantically thumbed through pattern books. She chose a pattern for a long sheath, sleeveless, scoop neckline, with a contrasting panel down the front—not too intricate, nor difficult to sew. The fabric she chose was velvet—dark blue for the dress and white for the panel. She cut and sewed late into the night all week to finish it. Friday evening, she carefully pressed the finished dress and tried it on. She pinned a silver and pearl brooch on one side. She was pleased with the reflection in the mirror. The rich color was becoming, the style suited her petite figure, making her appear taller. She decided she would put up her hair for more height.

Rory came to get her on Saturday night, and she noticed his eyes light up when he saw her. She was happy that she pleased him. She knew no one at the party, but Rory introduced her to his co-workers and their spouses or dates, and she was soon having a good time.

They filled plates at the buffet table that was filled with delicacies, and took cups of punch, probably containing vodka, and sat with two other couples, chatting as they ate, and listening to the band playing dance music.

They danced for hours, and they danced well together. They grew more confident and even tried some intricate steps. Rory asked the band to play their song, and they did, twice. Amanda wished the night would go on forever—that she could continue to be held in Rory's arms, and move to the music. Too soon, they were dancing the last dance, and Rory whispered endearments in her ear. The music ended and they were back on earth. As they walked to the car, Amanda discovered that her feet hurt. It was snowing, and they held onto each other as they slipped on the ice. The windshield was covered with ice, too, and Rory scraped as Amanda sat, shivering in her light evening wrap, willing the engine to warm quickly so she could turn on the heater. Rory climbed into the car and rubbed his hands together to restore the circulation. His hair was frosted with flakes of snow, and a lock fell over one eye, releasing icy drops onto his cheek. They looked at each other and began to laugh. They laughed until the car was warmed by their breath, and still they laughed. It seemed to well up from deep within them, where they communed with each other. At last they stopped, spent, and Rory looked at Amanda with mock bewilderment.

"Amanda, I don't think we're in Kansas any more!" he said.

They were strangely quiet on the way home. Yet Amanda felt closer to Rory than ever before. They kissed good night just inside her door. This kiss was different somehow—more than physical. She turned in her bed, unable to sleep. Her whole being seemed to vibrate with new life. What had happened? She did not know. It was as though they had touched another dimension. The outward events were ordinary enough, and they had only had two or three small cups of punch.

"We are living in a real world, an imperfect world, not a fairyland," she said softly into the darkness, "Rory's not perfect, and certainly I'm not." But for a few minutes, in the car, perfection ruled. Rory was perfect in every way, and she had felt herself being freed of imperfection—selfishness, bitterness, envy—every negative was stripped away. She didn't understand but she knew that she and Rory had been in a higher realm, and the bond between them was stronger than ever. She lay in wonder for hours before falling asleep.

She was mystified all the next day. When Rory arrived to accompany them to church, she kept studying him, trying to determine if he was different or if he had felt as she had the night before. He seemed much the same, although there was no teasing of the children after church, and he treated Amanda with great tenderness. Their eyes seemed to meet more often. She decided not to mention her experience. What could she say? She couldn't explain it to herself, certainly not to another. She stored it in her heart, but she never forgot.

The next weekend, the five of them made Christmas cookies: sugary cut-outs, gingerbread men (and women), cookies with dates and nuts, and exotic spices; buttery Spritz shaped into trees, and wreaths, and reindeer.

A favorite evening was when Amanda made candy: fudge, divinity, and date loaf. She was not expert at candy-making, but she allowed the children to scrape the pans, and they proved that her efforts were edible.

19

For unto us a child is born

(Isaiah 9:6)

On Christmas Eve, Amanda prepared clam chowder and Italian bread for supper, a tradition of several years, followed by a sampling of cookies and candies.

After eating, the children were allowed to open some of their gifts. The rest would be taken to Grandma and Grandpa's. Rory helped Amanda retrieve packages from her closet. The children shrieked as they each unwrapped large triangular shapes revealing shiny metal sleds. Rory promised to take them for a trial run the following week. Tinker was included in the fun. There was a wrapped can of tuna under the tree for him, and Amanda put half of it in his dish. He would have the other half Christmas morning. Tinker tried to hurry the process, with loud meows, as soon as he saw the can. Elizabeth stuck a big red bow on his head. He immediately pawed it off, yowling at her, and pushed the mangled bow under a chair.

After the wrappings had been put away, Amanda asked Rory to read the Christmas story from the Gospel of Luke. Amanda lit candles and turned the lamps off. They sat in the glow of the candles and the bright tree as Rory read, in his clear tenor voice, the familiar story of God leaving heaven to come down to men on earth as the baby Jesus. When Rory finished, he closed the Bible. They sat quietly several minutes sensing the presence of the Lord in the room.

"The story is new every year. I never tire of hearing it," said Amanda softly, breaking the silence. "He loves us so much."

She put an album of Christmas carols on the stereo and they listened as the story was retold in song. They sang along now and then. When the record stopped, Amanda turned it to the other side and told the children to get ready for bed. They would leave very early the next morning.

It had seemed most practical for Rory to stay overnight. He would take Elizabeth's room and Elizabeth would sleep with her mother.

When Amanda was sure the children were asleep, she quietly performed one of the tasks she enjoyed most at Christmas time—filling the Christmas stockings she had made years ago. Rory was eager to help. She retrieved hidden bags and filled each stocking with an orange, an apple, some nuts in the shell, and brightly wrapped candies shaped like bells and ornaments. They stuffed a few small items down the sides: red and green pencils with the printed message *Jesus Loves Me*, hair clips for Elizabeth, new combs for Matthew and Joshua, and a tiny toy for each. A fat red and white candy cane was placed to just peep out of the top of each stocking. They carefully propped them against branches at the base of the tree. Lastly, Amanda shut Tinker in the basement, despite his protests, knowing from past experience that his curiosity would lead him to paw inside the stockings.

That finished, Rory took Amanda in his arms. "This is one of the best evenings I've ever had. I am so glad I met you, and I am part of your life...." His voice broke. "I love you so much!" He held her tightly and she held him, her head pressed to his chest.

"I love you, too," she said in a slightly muffled voice. "I thank Jesus for bringing you to me."

He tightened his arms. They stood, thus, several minutes then Rory released her, kissed her tenderly, and said he would see her in the morning.

When he was safely in Elizabeth's room, Amanda gathered bags from filling the children's stockings, and tiptoed to her bedroom. She had debated how to go about filling a stocking for Rory without his knowing, and without waking Elizabeth. The best idea she had was to sit on the floor of her closet with a flashlight. This she did, hoping she hadn't dropped evidence on the closet floor. In addition to the goodies, she included a ballpoint pen—large point and with a diameter the size of her thumb, just as Rory liked. Finished, she stuffed the mostly empty bags in a corner, and tiptoed down the hall to the bathroom to prepare for bed. It was very late and they would have to rise early in the morning—this morning, she corrected in her head, after glancing at her watch.

Long before dawn, Amanda was in the kitchen making coffee and preparing a traditional small tray of hot chocolate and banana bread spread with cream cheese and red currant jelly. The children had been taught to stay in their beds until she woke them with this bit of nourishment before they began on the treats in their stockings. First she woke Rory, who had agreed to take photographs, with a Merry Christmas, before giving him a kiss and a cup of coffee. She then returned to the kitchen, turning on the album of carols as she walked through the living room. She carried the tray to the small play table in Elizabeth's room, then woke the children with similar kisses and greetings. Elizabeth had been fast asleep, but Matthew and Joshua were sitting up in bed, waiting. They eagerly went to the little table and devoured the contents of the tray, knowing the best was yet to come. Then, with Rory walking backwards down the hall, camera aimed and clicking at intervals, the children marched to the living room. Amanda brought up the rear. The children dived for their stockings and Rory continued to snap photographs, taking breaks to sip his coffee.

With everyone occupied, Amanda slipped back to her bedroom, then entered the living room with her hands behind her back. She went to Rory and held out the stocking.

"This seems to have been left here for you," she said. Rory slowly stretched out his hand, and took the stocking.

He held it in front of him, staring at it, and then sat in a chair.

Amanda stood, perplexed, wondering what was wrong. She crouched on the floor beside him. "Honey? Are you all right?" she asked.

He gave her a strange look. "The stocking … when did you.… I didn't expect.…" He stopped in confusion.

Amanda jumped up and sat in his lap. "Oh, Rory! Merry Christmas, Sweetheart!" She threw her arms around him and smothered his face with kisses.

He began to respond and when a smile broke out on his face, she said slowly and distinctly: "Merry, Merry Christmas, Honey. I love you."

"Merry Christmas, and I love you, too," he replied, and now a grin split his face.

The silence in the room drifted into Amanda's consciousness and she looked at the children. They were sitting on the floor; stockings and candy spread in their laps, and staring at her and Rory.

She jumped off Rory's lap. "We must get going. Get dressed kids, and bring your bags to the front door. You may take your stockings with you. You too, Rory!" she said.

Everyone raced around and soon the car was packed. By 6:30, Rory and the children were in the car and Amanda stood at the door, checking that everything had been packed. Tinker stood in the middle of the living room giving her a baleful stare with his yellow, unblinking eyes. He had been provided with extra food, including the tuna, ample water, and a clean litter box, but he made it clear that nothing would appease him for being left behind. Amanda gave him instructions to guard the house well, and shut the door, making sure the lock snapped.

As soon as they were out of the city, the children nodded off. The sunrise revealed a cloudless sky. It was cold, with snow covering the fields, meadows, and ditches. The roads, however, were dry—a beautiful Christmas Day. The mountains gleamed in their covering of pristine white, touched with gold where the sun's rays struck.

"What beauty God put on this earth for us to enjoy," Amanda said, smiling at Rory.

He smiled in agreement. "Try to get a picture. Should I stop, or can you take it from the window?"

Amanda located the camera at her feet. She rolled down the glass and focused on the spectacular view rushing by on her right. The cold wind blew tendrils of hair and nipped at her ears. She snapped the shutter several times, then quickly rolled up the glass. "Brr," she said, shivering and rubbing her fingers. Her cheeks and nose were rosy and her hair stuck out in all directions.

Rory laughed at her, "You look about twelve years old."

She wrinkled her nose at him and turned down the sun visor to check herself in the mirror, combing her hair into order. About midway, they stopped for coffee and cocoa. Back in the car, Rory played the harmonica—mostly Christmas songs, and, as always, he played "Shenandoah" and ended with "This Song's For You." This was the first trip they had made in Rory's new car, and while the back seat was small, the children liked its sportiness and urged Rory to use its powerful engine to the fullest on take-offs. They also enjoyed hearing the few tapes, over and over, until Amanda was sure they knew them by heart.

The children were permitted to indulge in the bounty of their stockings and Rory shared his with Amanda. It was a pleasant journey. They arrived at the farm just before noon.

Greetings were lavish and lengthy, and after overnight bags were carried upstairs, it was time to prepare for the festivities. Dinner was planned for five o'clock. A platter of sandwiches was placed on the counter for those who could not wait. More family members arrived, and children of all ages ran, tottered, and crawled underfoot. Christmas carols from the radio were drowned out by greetings, commands, cries, laughs, and other utterances of the human voice. In short, a cacophony of sound filled the house, if one took the trouble to listen to the whole. But no one did, each being involved in a small cell of activity.

Amanda had brought several food offerings, as had the other women. All were unwrapped, exclaimed over, and added to the considerable array Catherine began to remove from her refrigerator and shelves.

The expanded dining table, set buffet style, displayed the bounty. An arrangement of holly, pine, and tiny ornaments marked the center and caught the eye, which then could move in any direction, taking in the array of artistically arranged and garnished trays and platters of sliced ham, turkey, and savory meat balls in sauce, molded salads suggestive of Joseph's coat of many colors, multi-shaped and flavored breads, mushrooms and crisp celery stuffed with aromatic goodness, sweet potatoes dressed with slices of fruit, olives, and pickles.

On the sideboard, pies, cookies, candies, and nuts surrounded a footed crystal plate holding a coconut-covered angel cake. A fat red candle rested in the center hole and red frosting proclaimed the reason for the feast: "Happy Birthday, Jesus."

The large, sweet-smelling tree in the living room, topped with an angel dressed in white and gold, arms outstretched as though proclaiming the "Good News," was almost engulfed by packages. These packages were all sizes, shapes, colors, and patterns, adorned with ribbons, tiny pine cones, and candy canes, and increased in number and volume, as late-arriving members of the family added their contribution. Greeting cards, standing stiffly like heralds, covered small tables. In combination, it was a banquet for the five senses.

Amanda felt a little lost in the melee, having spent Christmas with only her small family in attendance for a decade. She wondered how Rory was faring, and went to look for him. She had no idea where her children were, but correctly deduced that an aunt or uncle would be supervising. She finally found Rory, in company with James, Ed, and David inspecting James' new self-propelled combine. She stood watching, unseen. *Machinery*, she thought, *it attracts some men as bikini-clad beauties attract others! I'm glad Rory is in the machinery category!* She smiled and retraced her steps, hoping that last thought was true.

At last everyone had arrived and all was ready. James asked Amanda, as the eldest child, to give the blessing. She began, her voice faltering as her heart filled with love for God, for Rory, her children, her parents, her brothers and sisters. She continued: "Father, thank You for this Day of Celebration of the birth of Your Son, Jesus. Thank You for loving us enough to send Him to us. Thank You for letting us be together today. Bless the hands that worked to bring it about, and bless the food. Let this celebration fill our souls, as well as nourish our bodies. In Jesus' name. Amen."

Mothers began filling tree-patterned paper plates for the younger children, seating them on small chairs, and in high chairs scattered in various corners. Older children next, some sitting on the floor, with plates piled high, others preferring the picnic table outdoors, as the day had warmed considerably. Lastly, the adults, good-humoredly finding places wherever they could. Rory and Amanda slipped outside, away from the overheated house and incessant noise.

Amanda had paused momentarily while standing in line, thinking of the days of salad and fruit that would follow this indulgence. She had deliberately squelched the twinge of conscience and spooned a sampling of most everything onto her plate. Now she stared at its roundness. Rory's was mounded even higher than hers. They ate heartily, oohing over bites they found especially tasty, and washing it down with Catherine's holiday punch.

The sun had almost disappeared when they finished, and the air had turned cool. Back inside, they found a vote was being taken to open the presents now, and have dessert later. It passed with only a few dissenting juvenile nays. The older children began to pass out gifts, while Amanda helped the women clean up some of the clutter. They sacked trash and took it to the incinerator, put silverware to soak in the sink, covered chilled dishes and stacked them in the refrigerator. The rest would wait.

When Amanda left the kitchen, she spotted Rory sitting on a straight chair in the corner. Three or four presents had been placed on the floor in front of him. She couldn't read his face. Bewildered? Bemused? But why should he be? She started towards him, but a package was being held out to her and she took it, smiling at the little Santa's helper.

The noise level mounted as children opened their gifts, hopes and dreams realized. Gag gifts for the adults whose names were drawn in November were preferred. These resulted in teasing and sometimes mild embarrassment. This family was not for the timid or withdrawn—or prim, either, though the badinage was always in good taste (Catherine allowed nothing off-color within her house or hearing).

The last gift was unwrapped and admired, and fathers collected filled cartons and bags to put in the car, leaving each child with a treasure or two, while mothers sorted through wrappings for a few keepsakes, and put the rest in a large waste can.

Then lights were turned off, leaving the area in semi-darkness, lit by the tree and candles. Relative quiet descended as everyone found a place to sit. Catherine entered holding the birthday cake, candle glowing, and Sue and Jeanette led the singing of the simple "Happy Birthday Song," honoring Jesus.

Near bedlam again, as fresh plates were brought out, and desserts chosen. Mother voices mounted, in sharp counterpoint to high-voiced youngsters, protesting the restraint on sweets.

By nine, the rooms were in relative order and several families were gathering drowsy children and scattered belongings. "Thank you!" "See you soon!" and "Merry Christmas!" filled the air, as they drove away. The remaining children were allowed an extension to their usual bedtime, and they busied themselves with their new toys. James and Catherine, tired and happy, sat in their easy chairs, watching a Christmas program on television, and discussing the day.

The young adults cleared the dining table for a board game, deciding, after lively banter, on a game of deduction. They played, interrupted by jokes, anecdotes, and putting children to bed, until midnight. After the others left for their own homes (James and Catherine had retired hours ago), Amanda divided the last of the coffee between Rory's cup and hers, and they sat in front of the tree, slightly bedraggled now, but still bravely sporting its spirals of lights. They sipped the slightly bitter brew and nibbled on cookies. Amanda sighed with contentment and marveled at how much pleasure could be packed into one day. Praise to the One whose birthday they celebrated, joy at being here, the sparkle in the eyes of her children, and Rory by her side, sharing it all—she wanted to sing, to shout, "Life is so good!" She looked at Rory, sitting silently beside her.

"Did you have a good time today?" she asked, thinking he was more quiet than usual.

"I had a good time," he said slowly, taking her hand. "I just didn't expect …" he stopped.

Amanda squeezed his hand. "It was a bit overwhelming, even for me."

Rory didn't answer. He was seemingly lost in thought.

"Honey?" Amanda said, and placed her other hand on his knee. "Are you all right? Did someone say something?"

Rory shook his head and gave her a small smile. "No, except for your Aunt calling me by your ex-husband's name!"

"Oh! I didn't hear her do that."

"Your Dad did. He was angry with her. I told him it didn't

matter and your Aunt apologized. It was rather comical, really."

"It didn't upset you, then?"

"No, it was just a mistake. I felt sorry for your Aunt. She was very embarrassed."

"I'm glad you weren't upset, Honey. It's bound to happen once in a while. So why were you so pensive just now?" She paused. "What else happened?"

"The gifts … I didn't expect any gifts. From you, I thought, but … there was one from David and Debbie, your other brother, your sister, and your parents. There was one from the kids.… I didn't know what to do. I thought it was a mistake—that they weren't meant for me. When you drew names at Thanksgiving, you asked me to draw, too. And I did, and I bought a gift for Ed. I drew his name. I expected to get one gift, from that. I read the tags—over and over—they had my name on them, but.…"

"Oh, Sweetheart.…" Amanda fought back tears, and kissed Rory, gently. "Of course the presents were for you! You're part of the family now. Everyone wanted to welcome you especially, as the newest member of the family, and to let you know that they care about you." She smiled, and touched his cheek. It felt moist to her finger. "I love you, Rory. I love you so much. All our Christmases will be like this. I promise."

He smiled back at her, then sat holding her hand, still thoughtful.

"Was there more you can tell me?" Amanda asked, gently.

He turned and took her other hand, holding them cupped in his. For the first time since Amanda had met him, he seemed to be at a loss for words. She sat quietly, looking at his face, waiting.

"The cake. I had never actually thought of Christmas being Jesus' birthday. I mean I knew it was to celebrate the birth of Christ. But it didn't mean anything to me. It was just words. The birthday cake—suddenly it became real to me. Jesus was an actual baby. He was born, He lived on this earth, and He died on the cross. It isn't just a story, just words in the Bible, that you say because it's Christmas time. For the first time, I understand what Christmas is."

Amanda's eyes were shining. "That's wonderful! I'm so happy for you! Thank you for telling me this. The food, the presents, the decorations—they're all a lot of fun, and I'm positive that Jesus wants us to have fun. But the real Christmas story—the meaning—is that Jesus came to earth as a baby because He loved us enough to leave heaven, come down here to this world with evil in it, grow up enduring all the problems we have in life, and at last, of course, to die, horribly, on a cross—all for us. We should celebrate!"

"Well, I know Christmas will never be the same for me after this. And I'm so glad to have been a part of it here with you," he told her, and put his arms around her. They sat holding each other until sleep almost overcame them, then they tiptoed quietly upstairs to their separate rooms.

They had planned to leave early the next morning, but what with breakfast, packing, and lingering good-byes, it was mid-morning when they drove away, waving until the car turned the corner.

The children soon dozed, rocked by the car's motion, and warmed by the sun streaming through the windows. Amanda turned to look at them several times. They were growing up, and, as myriads of mothers before her, she wondered where the years had gone. They were no longer her babies. Soon they would be out in the world, on their own, and she knew she would be powerless to protect them from hurt. *Jesus, watch over them, please. Keep them safe. They are so precious to me—and even more so to You. Thank You for trusting me with them for a time.*

Rory touched her arm. "Why so serious?" he asked.

"I was thinking what a blessing children are ... well, most of the time," she said, endeavoring to cover her emotion. "Would you like some coffee?" she asked and reached for the thermos.

"Sounds good, and a cookie or two if you can find them."

The children woke, hungry and thirsty. Amanda unwrapped sandwiches, made that morning from left-over turkey and ham, and poured punch into paper cups.

The children, being gastronomically satisfied, played with new toys, and looked through books they had received. Rory played carols and their favorite tunes on his harmonica. Amanda watched the scenery come and go—a glittering landscape basking in the warm sunlight, more beautiful than any man-made decorations. The music and soft voices lulled her and she nodded now and then. They were home by mid-afternoon.

Tinker greeted them, as they walked in, with voluble protests at being abandoned. It was good to be home.

The next few days were very cold. There was only a dusting of new snow, but the streets were icy from earlier melting. Driving was treacherous, even with the new studded tires on Amanda's car. Rory brought her a heater to put under the hood and she plugged it into an outlet in the garage each night to keep the battery working. It was too cold to go sledding, too cold to play outside for more than a few minutes. Amanda had tried to set up a schedule that would keep the children occupied while she was at work. They met her each evening at the door complaining about each other, about the forced inactivity, about complaining. Amanda was at her wit's end and prayed for sun and warmth—and for school to resume. Rory came over each night, and they all played games. Rory even rough-housed with the boys on occasion, so they could vent some energy, but Amanda didn't approve of it in the house, fearing for lamps and tables, as well as bruises from the hard floor. She kept quiet, though, most of the time, as they all seemed to enjoy it and the children were more amenable to going to bed without a fuss.

20

A merry heart doeth good like a medicine

(Proverbs 17:22)

They planned a quiet New Year's Eve. They would have finger food, then watch the fireworks that would be set off from the top of Pike's Peak, an annual event. Amanda agreed that the children could stay up to see the New Year "come in" and they argued about what they should do when the clock struck twelve, finally settling on blowing party whistles from the front walk.

Rory arrived about seven, tired and pale. He said he hadn't felt well all afternoon and blamed it on something he had eaten. He declined a glass of punch, saying he might have something later, and slumped into a chair. Amanda placed her palm on his forehead. It seemed a bit warm. She helped him remove his shoes and move to the couch, and wrapped a large afghan around him. He promptly fell asleep. She allowed the children to take filled plates and cups to the play table in Elizabeth's room.

Amanda sat in the living room reading and listening to the stereo. Every so often she looked at Rory. He seemed to be sleeping peacefully. *He's probably just tired and a good nap will set him right*, she thought.

At nine, Amanda moved the Christmas tree away from the window, turned out the lights, and she and the children watched the fireworks. It was a clear night and the colors glowed in the blackness high above the city lights. It lasted about an hour, ending with perhaps a dozen bursts set off at the same time—a beautiful sight that left them awed.

Rory slept on and when Amanda gently touched his brow, she thought it was hotter than before. His sleep was now punctuated with little jerks and moans. He roused when Amanda called his name and shook his arm (remembering to stand well behind him) and swallowed the aspirin she handed to him. He scarcely opened his eyes.

The children played games in the other room, between refurbishing their plates and cups. They crept silently past Rory, and stole glances at Amanda, astonished that she had not said that was enough punch. Amanda hid a smile, and did not interfere, hoping Tinker would take care of spilled food, and that the children would not wake later with stomach aches.

A few minutes before midnight, she called them. They sat on the floor, trying to hide yawns, watching an orchestra in New York on the TV counting down the minutes. At two minutes to twelve, she helped them don jackets and caps, and handed each a whistle. They hurried outside, allowing a balloon of icy air inside, and blew noisily on the whistles for less than five minutes, then rushed back inside, red-cheeked and shivering, and a little puzzled that this was all there was to it. Amanda gave them hot chocolate and sent them to bed.

Rory had not stirred, but he opened his eyes when she called his name, and reluctantly allowed her to stick a thermometer in his mouth. It registered an alarming 103 degrees. Rory forced himself to his feet, and said he had to go home.

Amanda took his arm firmly. "Forget that, Mister!" she said and led him to her bedroom. She helped him remove his outer clothing and climb into bed. His protests were feeble. She went for another blanket and more aspirin. Rory obediently swallowed the aspirin and laid his head back on the pillow with his eyes closed. Amanda wiped his flushed face with a cloth rinsed in cold water, touched his forehead with her lips, gathered her night things and left, closing the door. She slept, fitfully, on the couch, rousing once to give Rory more pills and again bathed his face.

At eight the next morning, Elizabeth woke her and she sat up stiff and disoriented. The children made their own breakfast of juice, cereal, and toast, while Amanda checked on Rory. His temperature was still 103 degrees. He downed aspirin and a few swallows of orange juice, while apologizing for being so much trouble. Ignoring that, she bathed his face and arms with cool water, tucked the blankets under his chin and kissed his cheek.

"You rest," she ordered. I'll be back soon."

She told the children that Rory probably had the flu, and that they were to stay out of the room, and were to play as quietly as possible. They could watch the New Years Day parades on television.

Amanda found a chicken in the freezer compartment and decided to make soup, having heard it called "Jewish penicillin," though she didn't know what other ingredients it should have. She put the chicken in a pan of cold water to thaw. The children helped her tidy the house during commercials.

When the parades ended, they went outdoors. The day was sunny, not too cold. A few inches of crusted snow covered the ground. Tinker hated snow, but refused to shirk his self-appointed task of taking care of the children, and sacrificed dignity for duty. He walked jerkily, shaking his paws as if a novice puppeteer had him on a string.

When the chicken thawed, Amanda set it to stew with lots of onion and garlic and some carrots and celery. The savory aroma soon filled the kitchen, raising her spirits. Rory was sleeping when she crept into the room. She took her jacket and purse from the closet and Rory's house key from his pants and tiptoed out. She turned the chicken to low and went out the back door. The children were making a snowman, and she told them she was going to get some medicine for Rory and would be right back. They were to stay outdoors.

Sunday. New Year's Day. Amanda wondered if she could find a store open. A few blocks away, however, a large chain supermarket was doing a brisk business. There was an entire section of flu remedies, and she spent several minutes reading labels. They seemed almost identical to her, and all unreadable. She chose three at random and wrote a check for an amount that shattered her budget. At Rory's house, she found clean pajamas, underclothes and toiletries, and shoved them into a paper bag.

Back home, the children complained of being hungry and cold. She told them to come inside, leaving the snow outside. She grabbed one package of pills and went to her bedroom. Rory was awake. His eyes were clouded, but he gave her a weak smile. Amanda showed him the pills and he dutifully swallowed some with a little juice. The bedclothes were twisted around and under him like a poorly constructed cocoon, and she tugged at them.

"How did this happen?" she asked him.

"Don't know," he muttered and tried to move his legs and arms to help her, only tangling himself further.

She managed to get him covered, and kissed his cheek. It was hot, but seemed no worse. She put his pajamas on the dresser, saying he could get into them when he felt like it, and that his toothbrush, razor, and other things were in the bag by the closet. His eyes were closed as she tiptoed out and softly closed the door.

In the kitchen, Matthew was sweeping clumps of snow out the back door with a broom. Joshua was behind him trying to wipe up muddy puddles with a bath towel. Elizabeth was sitting on the floor, vainly trying to remove her icy boots without using her hands. Tinker was swishing his tail in disgust.

Amanda started to remonstrate, decided against it, and turned to the stove. She turned the burner to reheat the soup and removed the chicken pieces to a chopping board. After removing the bones and dicing the chicken, she returned the pieces to the pot. She heated milk for cocoa and dumped crackers in a basket, ignoring the drama behind her, except for surreptitious glances over her shoulder. When she did turn to tell them lunch was ready, Matthew was stuffing jackets, stocking caps, and mittens into the washer, which stood along the far wall. Joshua and Elizabeth had disappeared. Six dripping boots sat in puddles of their own making by the door. Joshua and Elizabeth returned, lugging wet bundles of clothing which they heaped on the washer. Joshua began punching at the mass with his fists, while Elizabeth yelled encouragement. They had not quite managed to subdue it when Matthew returned from changing his wet clothes. At the sight of the additional mess in his arms, Joshua and Elizabeth gave up and looked to Amanda for inspiration. Hands on her hips, she contemplated their dilemma. A mound of jumbled clothing sprawled on the washer, parts hanging down the side dripping like a wounded octopus.

"Good job, guys," she concluded. "Wash your hands for lunch."

They breathed audibly with relief and ran to obey. Amanda turned her back on the washer and filled bowls with soup. While the children ate, she strained broth into a mug and took it to Rory. He was better, at least he said so with a look that dared her to disagree, and hungrily sipped the hot liquid. She sat on the side of the bed, smiling at him.

"Would you like the radio on?" she asked. He nodded and she found a station playing soft music. "Are you warm enough?"

Another nod. A weak grin passed over Rory's face, when she told him about Tinker in the snow. She continued to chatter until he handed the mug to her. Only about half the soup was gone.

She adjusted the pillows and told him to rest. He didn't acknowledge her words. Apparently he was already asleep.

When the children asked about Rory, she told them he still must stay in bed and they must play quietly. She felt each one's head. *All normal,* she thought. She played games with them, read to them, and dispensed pills, juice, and soup to Rory until their bedtime. Matthew offered his bed to her, saying he could use a sleeping bag.

She hugged him and declined. After the children were in bed, she lingered in her bath until the water was cool. Then she wrapped herself in a warm robe and sat in the corner of the couch, her legs folded under her, and her Bible on her lap. She read Psalms for half an hour and prayed that Rory would be well by morning, and that she and the children would not become ill.

The next morning, she hurriedly dressed, got the children ready for school, gave Rory medicine and placed water and juice where he could reach them. She told him to call her at work if he needed her, and she would be back at lunchtime to check on him.

At work, she called Rory's office to let them know he was ill, and promised to keep them informed. She called the doctor who had treated Elizabeth when she had a sore throat, and explained the situation. He told her the symptoms appeared to be from the flu that was rampant in the city, and he would call the drug store. She could pick up a prescription in an hour or so. He warned her to bring Rory to his office if he wasn't better within twenty-four hours.

She was aghast when she walked into her bedroom at noon. Rory was bathed in sweat, and shivering. The blankets were tumbled on the floor. She helped him into the bathroom. When he insisted, "I can do this myself," she filled the sink with warm water, laid out washcloth, towel, and pajamas. She then turned her attention to the bed. She stripped off the sheets and smoothed on fresh ones, and found a spare pillow. She carried the soiled linen to the laundry area, washed her hands and heated the last of the broth, adding a few small chunks of chicken. She returned to the bedroom with a tray of soup, a few crackers, and the prescription medicine. Rory was back in bed, his hair was combed, and he gave her a wan smile. She told him she had talked to the doctor, and gave him the prescribed pills. He swallowed a few mouthfuls of soup, and Amanda settled him down in the bed and rearranged the covers. His head still felt hot to her touch.

"Will you be okay if I go back to work?" she asked, with a frown.

He insisted that he felt better and just wanted to sleep, and she reluctantly left. She left a note for Matthew to make sure that Rory took two of the prescription pills as soon as Matthew got home from school. He was to call her if necessary. He was not to stay in the sickroom long, and was to scrub his hands with soap as soon as he came out.

She called home at 3:30 and Matthew said Rory had taken the medicine and had told Matthew that he thought he was better. When she walked in after work, Rory was reclining on the couch, with pillows behind him, and his legs covered with an afghan. Elizabeth was coming from the kitchen with a glass of juice, and Matthew and Joshua were seated on the floor facing him.

"So—what's all this?" Amanda asked as she removed her coat.

"We're helping Rory get better," explained Elizabeth.

"I see," said Amanda. She handed her coat to Matthew, her purse to Joshua, and asked them to hang them in the closet.

"It's great to see you up," she said and blew him a kiss as he took the juice from Elizabeth's outstretched hand.

"It's the good nursing I'm getting," he said and winked at Elizabeth.

She watched, gravely, as he drank and then took the glass.

"We were quiet," offered Joshua, returning to the room.

"And we did our homework," added Matthew.

"I didn't have any homework," smirked Elizabeth.

"I'm proud of each of you," said Amanda.

Turning to Rory, she asked, "How are you feeling, really?" His face was pale and there was no sparkle in his eyes.

"Better, a little tired," he told her.

"I'll fix supper, then you get back in bed. You don't want a set-back."

"I thought I'd go home tonight, so you can have your bed back."

"No way, Sir!" she replied fiercely. "And don't argue. I'm stronger than you are right now."

She scrambled an egg and toasted bread for Rory, and started spaghetti sauce for the children's dinner. Rory sat up and ate about half of his food, then set the fork down. Amanda noticed the whiteness around his mouth and the slump of his shoulders and tenderly steered him to bed. She talked about trivialities for a few minutes as she again dispensed medicine. When Rory's eyes closed, she slipped out, leaving the radio on low.

She tucked the children into bed after their prayers and made up the couch for herself. Sleep came quickly but fitfully. Several times she walked down the hall and listened to Rory's steady breathing. About 3:00, she gave him more pills, and slept soundly until 6:00.

The next day was even more hectic than the day before. Rory's temperature was a little less than 103 degrees, which was an improvement. He took a small glass of juice with his medication. Amanda fed the children, helped them to get ready for school, and left for work.

At lunch time, she went home, finding Rory again bathed in sweat. He got into dry clothing while she changed the bed linens, warmed some canned soup and gave him his pills. He sat on the side of the bed and drank all the soup—a good sign. He seemed much better, but was very weak and slumped back on the bed after eating. She again left a note for Matthew and went back to work.

Rory stayed at Amanda's two days more, mustering his strength. He objected, but Amanda was obdurate, going so far as to hide his car keys. When she returned from work at the end of the fourth day, she found Rory and the children frying chicken for supper. They had even made corn bread. She smiled widely and said a quick prayer of thanks. Rory was well, and she and the children had escaped the illness.

They spent a happy evening. The food was delicious and appetites healthy. Amanda asked Rory to go slowly on the heavy food, but he dismissed her concern with a wave of his hand. He deferred to her demand that he stay one more night, rather than venture out into the frigid air, and he retired early. He left after breakfast the next morning, intending to go to work after a hot bath at his house. That evening, when he arrived at Amanda's, he was tired, but happy and healthy.

21

Make a joyful noise unto God

(Psalm 66:1)

That Saturday, they planned to go sledding. The children were ready and sitting on the couch, waiting for Rory to arrive. It was a chilly morning, and he came in rubbing his hands.

"Boy!" he said, "It's a great day for the race."

The children looked at him with interest. "What race?" asked Joshua, who was very interested in cars.

"The *human* race!" said Rory, with a gleam of mischief in his eyes.

The children laughed. "Yeah! It's a great day for the race." said Joshua.

They took the sleds to a hill a few miles up the pass. It was a clear, sunny day. Several inches of snow had fallen during the night. Snow plows, blue lights flashing, labored to clear the highway, spewing snow, and surrounding themselves in miniature blizzards, and creating icy hillocks on either side of the pavement. Pine boughs sagged with their white burdens, like tired sentinels. Travel was slow, but they arrived to find the hillside packed with sleds. The children's new sleds were fast—a few thrilling seconds down the hill, then slipping and sliding, the sled was man-handled to the top to repeat the cycle, over and over. Whoops, yells, and cries splintered the cold air. Little clouds of breath-fog followed behind the sledders, as they trudged up and flew down. Amanda was sledding with Elizabeth;, while Rory took turns partnering first with Joshua, then Matthew. After one tumble about half-way down the hill, which left Amanda and Elizabeth smothered in snow and laughter, Amanda realized her watch was not on her wrist. She began digging, frantically, at the site of the spill, dodging other sleds coming from above.

Rory came to help, and although they searched for almost half an hour, the watch was not found. Amanda was near tears, and furious with herself for not removing the watch, which was a graduation present from her parents. Rory tried to comfort her, and promised to get her another one. It was a sweet and generous gesture, and though Amanda loved him for it, she was not easily consoled. The sentiment far outweighed the loss of a timepiece. However, after a few minutes, she realized she was selfishly ruining the fun for the others, and asked Elizabeth to help her tow the sled up for another downhill ride.

By mid-afternoon, they were exhausted. They brushed snow from the sleds, as best they could, and stowed them in the trunk, along with soaked gloves, caps, and jackets, and headed home. Rory had started the engine when they reached the car, and the heater, now turned to high, warmed them, making them yawn. The children nodded off within a few minutes, and Amanda fought her drowsiness, so she could help Rory to stay alert on the icy road.

She made chili for supper; hot chocolate for Rory and the children, and a pot of tea for herself. Full and fit after their day, and content with their closeness, they sprawled in the living room until bedtime.

22

The word of the Lord endureth for ever

(1 Peter 1:25)

They had been attending church together for several months. The church was of contemporary architecture and had a beautifully furnished sanctuary. Behind the altar was an immense wooden cross, perhaps fifteen feet high. The choir loft filled the left side, the organist in front and slightly to the side. The pulpit was always draped with intricately embroidered cloths appropriate for the season, and the altar rail spanned the entire width. Pew benches were padded and covered in silky, rose-colored fabric. The members were friendly and had made them feel welcome from the beginning. Rory and Amanda had joined an adult church-school class, and the children were in classes appropriate for their ages. The minister was perhaps forty, personable and charismatic, a polished speaker, and his sermon topics were thought-provoking.

The sermon this Sunday was taken from the Gospels, recounting several miracles Jesus performed, including His turning water into wine at the wedding at Cana.

Amanda pondered, not for the first time, the meaning of this miracle and why it was included in God's Word. Dozens of miracles must have been omitted. She determined to search her Bible for answers when she got home. She enjoyed a glass of wine on occasion, as did Rory, and had, at times, been concerned at her enjoyment.

After lunch, Rory became engrossed in a football play-off game on television, the children were occupied, and she settled at the dining table with her Bible and a notebook. She found wine listed seventeen times in the small Concordance at the back of her Bible. She looked up the references and noted their context.

Judges and a Psalm say wine is that "which cheereth God and man," and that it is given by God and "maketh glad the heart of man." Another Psalm and Revelation refer to a cup of wine as being the wrath of God. Four were references to excess of wine and drunkenness causing woe, poverty, redness of eyes. In Ephesians, it says bishops should not be given to wine, and Peter speaks of an excess of wine in company with lasciviousness, lusts, and revellings, which the Christian is to leave behind. Proverbs suggests giving wine to those with heavy hearts, and Paul said a little wine was good for the stomach. Solomon said love is better than wine. Isaiah has an analogy about mixing water in the wine causing the deterioration of Israel. Isaiah states that Christ satisfies thirst like buying milk and wine without money, and Hosea says that a restored Israel has a scent like the wine of Lebanon.

Now, if she could only figure out what all this meant. She dismissed the theory that the wine mentioned in the Bible was merely grape juice—drunkenness is not caused by grape juice. It appeared to her that the sin of wine was in the excess unto drunkenness, as the *love* of money unto excess was sinful. In fact, wine appeared to be of use to gladden the heart, and even as medicine. She agreed, wholeheartedly, that love was better than wine. The analogies in Isaiah re buying wine without money and the scent like wine of Lebanon, she didn't fully understand, but they seemed to be on the positive side, rather than the negative. The trouble was, she was fully aware that drunkenness and alcoholism were enormous problems in today's society, as they apparently had been in Bible times. The excess use of wine and/or addiction to it was to be taken seriously.

Amanda asked the Holy Spirit to guide her into truth as was promised in Saint John. In the meantime, she would continue to enjoy an occasional glass of wine. "I believe an excess of most anything leads to it being a god, as forbidden in the First Commandment," she concluded.

23

All things work together for good

(Romans 8:28)

In early January, a letter arrived from civil service. An interview was arranged for Amanda with an Army unit within the city. She called to confirm the appointment. She was ecstatic and made arrangements to take off from work for personal business.

She became increasing nervous as she drove to the interview—she knew nothing about the military. A colonel, a major, and the colonel's secretary were waiting for her. They set Amanda at ease at once, and the interview resembled a conversation. After a while, she was told that they would let her know the outcome in two days. She explained that she would need to give notice at her present job, and they agreed that, if she was chosen, her start day could be in two weeks.

Amanda prayed on the way home, asking the Lord to please let the job be hers. She knew she was capable of handling the work duties, and the job paid better, had better benefits, provided room for advancement, and perhaps best of all, would be interesting and challenging.

Amanda had left Debbie's number with the Army secretary, and on Thursday morning, Debbie called her saying that the Army "wanted her." Amanda called to confirm at lunchtime, and gave notice that afternoon. Amanda said a prayer of thanks and called Rory. He was delighted she was to leave her present job, and told her they would celebrate with dinner out.

Her boss was not very gracious, and Amanda felt a little guilty, as she had been grateful when he hired her. She soon reasoned that she had given her best, not to mention the harassment. Amanda helped select and subsequently train a new secretary, and then it was her last day. Two of her co-workers took her to lunch and wished her well.

The new job was exhilarating, outside her orbit of experience, professional in tone. It produced, in Amanda, a sense of being involved with matters of importance. The first morning, she filled out various forms, including an application for a secret security clearance—heady stuff!

24

Therefore will I play before the Lord

(2 Samuel 6:21)

Also, in January, Rory took the children to the ski slope in the foothills. They rented skis and boots, and set out for the learners' slope. Amanda went along, but, being totally non-athletic, she played spectator. The boots were awkward—stiff and flat-bottomed, and Amanda laughed as the children tried to walk (she had almost as much trouble on the slippery trail in her sneakers). Rory got the children snapped into their skis, and began to show them some elementary moves. They fell, they slid, and mostly they giggled. It was great fun. Rory took the children several times, thereafter. Amanda usually stayed home, doing Saturday chores. They would return in high spirits, and Rory, who had skied for several years, said they were beginning to get the hang of it. In fact, he predicted that the boys would soon pass him up in expertise. Elizabeth was not quite as daring, but she enjoyed it.

The rapport between Rory and the children was increasing almost daily. Every facet of Amanda's life was sprinting toward perfection, a circumstance that rather alarmed her at odd moments, when doubts assailed her, springing perhaps from a Puritan sense of being unworthy. These doubts were purged from her thoughts at their birth. She knew they did not originate from her Father, who, having dispensed good things, would not then snatch them away.

"Thank You, Lord, for even if You chastise me, as I sometimes do my children, I know You will chastise me in love, and not destroy me. You have brought me out of the valley and into the heights. I can never praise You enough!" Every night she thanked God for Rory, for Matthew, Joshua, and Elizabeth, before sinking into restful sleep. She was receiving the peace that passeth understanding as she walked with her Friend. Her eyes sparkled, her step was jaunty, her God was alive and cared for her. Once she tried to express her joy to Rory and once again to the children, but words failed her. It was too new!

Amanda had been encouraging Rory to begin to take on the responsibility of being a step-father. He had not been enthusiastic, as his relationship with the children was going so well. But, to please Amanda, he began, slowly, to let the children know that he would soon be the head of the house. Amanda also had talked to the children about this several times. Now, Rory might say "Time for bed," "Keep the noise down," "Wash your hands" and such. For the most part, the children obeyed without question. There had been a few bumps: "You're not my boss," "You're not my dad," "You don't live here," and so forth. At these times, Rory was patient and explained that he loved them, that he soon would be their step-father, and that he would be living with them. He told them that being a step-father was new to him, and he was trying to learn how to be a good one. He asked for their help. He and Amanda discussed rules of discipline and agreed to present a united front to the children at all times. If one disagreed with the other's decision, it would not be mentioned in the presence of the children. There would be no, "I'll go ask Mama," or "Rory will let me," in this household.

Amanda had hoped the children would call Rory by a title

name. She had brought the matter up in an off-hand manner several times. The children had not responded. Rory told her not to push it, that it didn't matter what name they called him, but how they responded to him was the important thing. They continued to call him Rory, and Amanda resolved to forget her disappointment.

On Valentine's Day, Rory brought a large, ornate, heart-shaped box of chocolates and red carnations for Amanda. There were smaller heart-shaped boxes for the children. Amanda made Rory's favorite meat loaf for dinner, and cherry cake in the shape of a heart, decorated with whipped cream. After dinner, they played a board game until the children's bedtime. Amanda and Rory danced to stereo music for a while, then talked of matters only they cared about.

One evening, the children were in bed, and Rory was in class. He probably would not come by this late, though he might call. Amanda made a cup of tea and sat on the couch. She paused as she lit a cigarette, and knew she should study the use of tobacco as she had the wine. But how to begin? It was not, she was sure, mentioned in the Bible. It was a plant of the New World. Just to make sure, she checked the concordance in her Bible—not there, as she expected. She had no full concordance.

She very much enjoyed a cigarette at times, as now with the hot tea in the late evening. It was a relaxing ritual. She liked the taste after meals. It seemed to dilute the heavy flavor of food. During the awful days when her marriage was being destroyed, she had smoked a great deal. It was one way of coping with her nervousness and despair. Now she smoked much less, but she would like to quit. In fact, she had tried, but had not succeeded. Rory smoked occasionally, but less than she did. She had asked Jesus to take the habit and desire away, but it had not happened. Perhaps, down deep in herself, she did not want to quit. What could she do now? Her father had quit, after years of smoking cigars, and had told her to use her will power. She had been devastated when she realized she didn't have the necessary will power. She had considered herself to be strong in mind—more than the average person. There seemed no answer to her problem. She was totally discouraged.

The sound of the phone brought her out of her feeling of inadequacy. It was Rory. As always, his voice lifted her spirits immediately. He was working hard to get good grades, and Amanda was doing all she could to encourage him to go home after classes, instead of coming to her house. It was difficult for both of them. They talked a few minutes, then Rory said he was going to bed and would get up early the next morning to study. Amanda hung up the receiver and prepared for bed also.

"Abba Father," she prayed, "thank You for being with Rory while he studies. Help him to concentrate on what he is reading so early in the morning. Let me always be understanding, and never cross when he can't be here. And, Jesus, please help me to quit smoking. I know it isn't good for me. I can't quit on my own; I've tried." Tears came to her eyes as she thought, again, that she must be a very weak person. "Jesus, You have given me Your strength so many times, why do I not have it in this area?" She wiped the tears away with her hand, and took a deep breath. "I have so many things to thank You for; I am so truly blessed. Keep me, Rory, and the children in the arms of Your love, Lord. And help me to be a better child. Amen." She turned her damp pillow over and dwelt on the love of God streaming down on her. In a few minutes, she was asleep.

They had continued to visit back and forth with David and Debbie, sometimes for dinner, or to play games. Amanda and Debbie became good friends, confiding in each other. In February, Debbie arranged a surprise birthday party for David at a steak house, to be followed by dancing to a country music band. Three couples plus Rory and Amanda were invited. Debbie had told David to meet her at the restaurant after work, as a friend wanted to talk to him. The surprise was perfect. David's mouth gaped when he arrived at their table. The entire evening was a success. Amanda enjoyed the dancing and admitted the band was good, even though country music was not her favorite.

Elizabeth's birthday was next on the calendar—late February. Amanda made a strawberry-flavored cake with a tiny doll on top, dressed in fluffy blue frosting. She invited five little girls for Saturday afternoon. Rory took the boys to the ski slope. It was a cold day with a few flakes of snow falling, so the birthday activities had to be indoors. The little girls played games and gossiped. They admired the doll-cake and thought it great fun to eat a "dress" along with chocolate ice cream.

When Rory and the boys returned, they had hot dogs and French fries (Elizabeth's choice) and more cake and chocolate ice cream. Amanda and Rory gave Elizabeth a little gold medallion with her birthstone in the center, on a delicate chain. When Amanda tucked Elizabeth into bed, she noticed the chain around her neck, under her nightgown. Elizabeth gave her an exuberant hug and told her she would never forget that day. Amanda held her very tight for a long moment.

"Oh, Father," she prayed that night. "Thank You so much for the little girl You have given me. And the little boys, too. Help me to always take care of them, and teach them the way You want me to. Thank You for bringing Rory to me, to help me raise them, and for me, too. You know what I need, and Your Word says You will give me what is best for me. Thank You for loving me that much. I love You, too."

25

In all labour there is profit

(Proverbs 14:23)

Amanda looked at the grade report Rory held out to her. All B's! This had been a more difficult quarter. Rory was taking three classes: English, Speed Reading (which he had so much fun with) and Personnel Management. Amanda had feared it might have been too much with all the pressures of taking on a new family. She was thrilled.

"This is wonderful, Honey!" she said. "You have worked hard and it was worth it. We'll celebrate! I'll make your favorite dinner Friday night. What would you like?"

"That's easy—fried chicken, creamed potatoes and gravy, tomato and lettuce salad, your special rolls, and pecan pie with ice cream," he said, grinning.

"You'll have it," she said and kissed his cheek. "But we mustn't celebrate with that meal very often!"

"Why not?" he asked, puzzled.

"Because it must have at least 10,000 calories a serving!"

"Oh. I didn't think of that," he said, solemnly.

"Don't worry, once in a while won't hurt us, I guess. Then we'll have cottage cheese and lettuce all next week," she said and grinned mischievously.

"Oh, no! No cottage cheese. I'll just have the lettuce."

"Why do you not like cheese, other than American cheese?"

"Well," he said sheepishly, "on the troop ship going to Nam—I think there were 5,000 of us on that ship for twenty-one days—we stopped at Guam and everyone went ashore. We did what most soldiers do on leave. We drank beer—and we ate pizza. We got back on the ship early the next morning and sailed a short time later. We ran into a storm, and even that big troopship was like a little toy in the waves. You can imagine—5,000 guys in close quarters, seasick, with hangovers from beer, and full of pizza besides. That's why I don't like the smell of cheese." He gave her a look which said "you asked!"

Amanda grimaced. "Serves you right! But I do sympathize—a little—and I won't serve you any sharp cheese. But cottage cheese is mild, why don't you like it?"

"I don't know, it just reminds me of sour milk. Maybe it's the texture."

"Okay, when I make lasagna, which has ricotta or cottage cheese, I'll fix spaghetti for you—but you should try a bite or two of the lasagna. You might like it."

"I'll think about it," he promised.

While Amanda had been staying at David's last June, David had shown her house plans that he had drawn up. He and Debbie had purchased a five-acre lot outside of town, and they planned to build a house there, themselves (with some help from friends). David had finally got the plans approved and had a construction loan. He planned to dig the basement and pour the foundation as soon as the weather permitted. Rory and Amanda had visited the site north of the city. It had a great view of the mountains and they thought they might like to purchase a lot there someday. At any rate, they promised to help as laborers, although neither of them knew much more about carpentry than how to drive a nail. One Saturday morning in late March, they took the children to the house site to check on the progress. David was there with two friends. The basement walls were poured and the septic system was in. Actual construction would go quickly now. David could only work evenings and weekends, of course, as could most of his helpers. He was under pressure to complete the house in the time allotted by his construction loan.

Rory and Amanda spent most of each weekend on the site that entire month. David was an excellent carpenter, but Rory and Amanda were green as grass, as were some of the other helpers. David's patience was often stretched, but he kept his sense of humor. One morning, he and Rory were measuring and cutting 2x4s. Rory, tape measure in hand, was trying to determine the needed lengths, while David ran the electric saw.

"What is the measurement for this one?"asked David, "It has to be exact."

Rory checked his tape. "It's two marks past the eight feet and six inches," he called out.

"What?" yelled David in disbelief, "Wait a minute! Bring that tape here, Rory. I'm going to show you how to read it." He did and soon Rory was shouting measurements like: "We need two feet, three and three-sixteenths inches!" or "Cut the notch four and nine thirty-seconds!"

There were more similar incidents, but despite them, the house continued to rise out of the bare ground, and it passed every inspection. Even the children helped, stacking scrap materials, and avoiding falling into holes, dug for one purpose or another. It was great fun, as well as hard work, and a source of satisfaction as the results of their efforts were clearly visible at the end of the day.

26

Wives, submit yourselves unto your own husbands

(Ephesians 5:22)

Amanda and Rory had looked at rings in almost every available jewelry store in the city. In early March, they chose medium wide bands of yellow gold, etched with ovals in white gold, with narrow filigree edges.

When they first discussed their wedding with their minister, Dr. Clay, in January, he told them he would require four counseling sessions before the ceremony. They made appointments for the last two weeks of March and the first two weeks of April.

At the first session, they were apprehensive and sat on the edges of their chairs, not knowing what to expect. The minister put them at ease with a few mild jokes. He then began to draw them into conversations on various topics. During the four periods, they discussed religious beliefs, finances, and the physical relationship in marriage.

At one point, the minister gave them a compatibility test (at least Amanda and Rory assumed that's that it was for), using Rorschach ink blots. Amanda's answers were predictable. It looked like a cloud, a flower, or a bunny. Rory's caused Dr. Clay to chuckle.

Rory's first comment was, "It's just a mirror image." When told, "Yes, but of what?" he said, "Siamese ink blobs," or "A squashed bug." They decided they had probably not passed this test. Then they were asked what their favorite colors were. Amanda's were blue and green, "The colors of the sky and grass and trees," she said shyly. Rory's response was orange and brown, and he had no further comment. They weren't told what this meant, and they thought they had probably failed this test, also. So much for the scientific view. After that session, Amanda and Rory laughed. They knew they complemented each other, regardless of the test results.

Amanda's children were discussed at length, and their position in the marriage, how Rory felt about them, and his commitment to them. Dr. Clay seemed satisfied with their responses. When the difference in their ages came up, Rory bristled and Amanda tensed. Rory tersely and firmly stated his view of that matter, and the minister smiled and went on to another topic.

At the last session, the minister explained the church's interpretation of Ephesians 6:22-33.

"The order is to be: Jesus, husband, wife, children. The husband is responsible to Jesus for his wife and children's welfare in the spiritual, physical, and mental realms. He is to treat his wife as Jesus treats the church—that is, to lay down his life for her, if necessary, and to cherish and respect her in all ways. He is never to use force, but to show her through love, what Christ has shown him. The wife is to submit to his authority in Jesus, so she is covered by the protection of the ordained order. She is to honor, uphold, respect, and cherish him. This did not mean that she was to be a slave to him, or that he was to be a dictator. Rather, that husband and wife were to discuss all issues and come to agreement. However, in the end, the husband's wishes must take precedence. The submission of the wife is in recognizing that her husband is responsible to Jesus for her well-being, and that of her children, and she is to assist him in all ways.

The children, then, were to submit to the authority of father and mother, and also were to honor their parents, as the parents were to cherish the children."

Amanda had never had this explained to her, and she thought the whole concept was wonderful. *Of course, it only works when husband and wife are committed to do Christ's bidding,* she thought. *And, I believe we are.*

At the end of the fourth session, Dr. Clay told them he would be happy to perform the marriage ceremony. He said they seemed to sincerely love each other, that they seemed committed to making the marriage work, that he felt they would work together to raise the children, and that their marriage should be successful. Amanda and Rory sighed with relief, and gave him a date of the first Friday afternoon in May. They told him it would be a very small wedding—just family.

"Father," Amanda prayed that night, "You brought Rory and me together. You have blessed our love for each other. Now, Your minister has made it *official*, here on earth. That's funny, to me, somehow. After all these months of getting to know each other, which You provided for, and we had to go through all the psychological testing, and so forth, when You had already ordained this marriage." She giggled. "Thank You for creating laughter; thank You for having a sense of humor. Thank You for what You have given me."

27

He is not here: for he is risen

(Matthew 28:6)

Amanda worked on Good Friday, but her heart wasn't in it. As always on this day, her emotions were on a roller coaster, and close to the surface. She constantly had visual pictures in her mind of Jesus being mocked and whipped, struggling to carry the heavy, crude cross, and she cringed. She would not allow herself to imagine the horror of His efforts to raise Himself so He could get a breath of air, as He hung on the cross. She would force the pictures from her mind and dwell on the "why"—why had God let this happen? And she was filled with gratitude.

When she arrived home she took aspirin for her headache and sat listening to the children tell about their day. School had dismissed at noon, and she had made an appointment for Tinker to get his annual shots, at the vet's across the street. She had instructed Matthew and Joshua how to wrap the cat in a towel to carry him. Unfortunately, Tinker's plan was somewhat different. He had resisted their inexperienced efforts to wrap him in a towel, and had hid under Amanda's bed. While Elizabeth wielded the broom from one side of the bed, Joshua and Matthew crouched on the other side ready to grab the fugitive, when he emerged. (Amanda silently gave them an "A" for thinking.) After several sweeps, Tinker jumped out.

"His tail looked just like an inside-out umbrella," said Joshua, in a hushed voice.

"He was mad, and we were scared," said Matthew.

"What did you do then?" asked Amanda, not sure she wanted to know, but seeing no visible scratches, she assumed it had turned out all right.

"I gave him a hot dog," said Elizabeth.

"She did, Mama, then she just wrapped him up in the towel, and we carried him to the vet," said Matthew.

"The vet wrapped him up for us to bring back home," said Joshua.

"Good job, kids!" said Amanda, smiling. "Where is Tinker now?"

"He's been under your bed ever since we got back," said Elizabeth. "You want me to get the broom, now? Matthew said to wait till you got home."

"I think we'll let him be for now," Amanda told her, and went to the kitchen to start supper. She smiled to herself several times as she peeled the potatoes. As she continued to prepare the meal, she thought again of the importance of the day. "Thank You, Jesus, for willingly going to that cross. Thank You for taking care of Matthew, Joshua, and Elizabeth, today. I'm so glad you have a sense of humor, too."

Rory knocked once and entered. "And thank You for that man coming through the door," she said, and went to greet him.

On Saturday, Amanda helped the children color and decorate eggs. She boiled twenty—six for each child, plus two spares in case of cracks. She mixed the colors: red, blue, green, and yellow, in coffee mugs, while the children used wax crayons to write names on the eggs: Matthew, Joshua, Elizabeth, Mama, Rory, and on the sixth, they wrote Jesus. After each child had finished an egg in each color, Amanda mixed them to make violet and orange. Slightly blurry designs of bunnies, chicks, and flowers completed their creations, which were then lovingly placed in bright baskets, lined with green paper grass.

When Rory arrived, the children proudly showed him their afternoon's work. He smiled when he saw his name on the eggs.

When the children were asleep, Rory helped Amanda put jelly beans, marshmallow eggs, and a large chocolate bunny in each basket. Amanda hid the baskets in the kitchen cupboard. When Rory left, she filled another basket for Rory and put it away.

Amanda woke early on Easter morning. The most exhilarating morning in the whole year—more exciting than Christmas and birthdays. She lay watching the first rays of the sun climb over the roof of the house behind hers. Her thoughts sped back in time to a morning almost 2,000 years ago. Mary Magdalene trudging along a rocky path, overwhelmed with sorrow, anxious to complete the burial rites for a man who had brought her out of despair, and given her hope. Now the hope was gone, slain, along with the man. She must have relived the horror of seeing that man hanging on the cross, a taunting mob at his feet. Probably, she then, as Amanda did now, felt her own breathing constricted by pain. Amanda forced her thoughts to leap ahead. Then Mary Magdalene's surprise at finding the stone not covering the opening to His tomb. The astonishment at hearing a young man inside the tomb say that Jesus was risen. She and the women with her had run, afraid, confused, from the burial place. Amanda ran with them in her thoughts, wondering what she would have been thinking at such an astounding story.

The unsurpassed joy Mary Magdalene must have felt when He appeared to her. Amanda's breathing became rapid. "He's Alive! He has risen!" This glorious day, to be relived each year, rejuvenated Amanda as no other. Joy filled her until she felt she would burst. She jumped out of bed whispering, "He's Alive!" and all that this meant to her flashed through her mind. Easter—the promise that no matter what happened to her on this earth, her life would end in victory.

She could climb mountains today! That feeling clung to her as she slipped on her robe and went to the kitchen to start the coffee, scramble eggs, and make toast (her bow to nutrition preceding the inevitable chocolate binge), and remained with her as she entered Matthew and Joshua's room, then Elizabeth's, to kiss them awake crying "Happy Easter!" with such fervor that each child giggled, wondering what had happened to their mother.

The children ran to the table where the colorful baskets filled with treats waited beside each plate of eggs and toast. Amanda allowed then to chose three goodies before they were sent to dress for church.

Rory arrived and, after returning his greeting kiss, Amanda handed him the basket she had filled for him. His surprise was almost as great as it had been at receiving the Christmas stocking. His pleased look added to Amanda's already overflowing heart and she laughed with sheer joy.

The church was packed. The scent and sight of flowers—lilies, roses, and more—was impressive, as was the music. Old hymns with the message that changed the world: *He's Alive*! The sermon was shorter than usual, and much the same as Amanda's waking musings, though this time related eloquently by the minister.

Meditative silence, even from the children, filled the car on the way home. It was a good-to-be-alive day.

At the house, Amanda and the children changed into casual clothes—Rory removed jacket and tie, and rolled up his shirt sleeves—and ate the dinner Amanda had largely prepared the day before: ham, potato salad, rainbow-hued fruit salad, rolls, and strawberry shortcake. It was a celebration of the renewing of their inner spirits, and a renewal of the earth, with the coming of spring.

Rory helped Amanda clear the kitchen, then stretched out on the couch for a short nap, while Amanda went to her bedroom to rest. The children were in the backyard, their play enhanced by the warm weather.

Later, Amanda and Rory listened to music and made plans for their wedding. After a light supper—Amanda forced the children to eat a few bites, hoping it would dilute the chocolate—they spent a quiet evening together watching television. Amanda's prayers that night were without mindful thought—simple "thank You's," straight from her heart, rose steadily until she fell asleep.

28

O taste and see that the Lord is good

(Psalm 34:8)

Neither Amanda nor Rory had vacation time coming, so they planned the wedding for a Friday afternoon. They would have Saturday away, and return home Sunday evening.

"Where shall we go on our honeymoon?" asked Rory. The children were in bed and Amanda and Rory were sitting on the couch. Amanda was going over her lists.

"We won't have much time. All day Saturday, then be back here Sunday night," said Amanda. "Mama said she and Daddy would stay with the kids."

"Would you like to go to Denver? There are many places to visit—museums, art galleries—you would like that—movies, if we want, nice restaurants."

"Denver sounds fine. Not too much traveling. Yes, I would like that. Where shall we stay?"

"You leave that up to me—I'll surprise you."

"I like your surprises!"

"Someday, we'll have a real honeymoon," Rory promised.

"Of course we will, we'll have lots of them," Amanda agreed.

She set her lists aside as Rory wrapped an arm around her and drew her close.

"Do you want to have more children?" asked Rory.

Amanda was startled. "Do you know, I have never given it a thought! Do *you* want more children?"

It would be nice to have a baby with you."

"Yes. I would like that, too." She thought a moment. "I think we should wait awhile though—until Matthew, Joshua, and Elizabeth are very comfortable. In two or three years? Maybe one or two more?"

"Okay. One or two in two or three years." He drew her to her feet. "I'd better go. Only a couple more weeks, then I won't have to do this any more!"

Amanda was determined that the wedding would not put them into debt. Everything must be paid for. She found blank announcement-sized cards of good quality at a stationery store and heavy envelopes to fit. She wrote out announcements in ink for family members and a very few close friends.

Amanda pored through pattern books again. She planned to make her wedding dress and one for Elizabeth, who would be the flower girl. Her choice for herself was street-length, with a raised waistline, a round neckline, and short sleeves. The skirt was tapered in front and gathered in back. She chose pale green silk to be sewn under white lace. Elizabeth's would be princess style—white lace over yellow. Amanda's colors would be green and yellow, the colors of spring—the new beginning of spring.

Catherine called, saying she would like to make Amanda's dress. Amanda was deeply touched and wrapped the material and pattern, after checking to see if it needed altering, and mailed them to her mother. Then she turned her attention to her trousseau. It would be simple. She made a rose-colored, flared skirt and bought a new blouse to go with it. The slacks Rory had given her would do for casual, and she found a new shirt to go with them. She bought white high-heeled sandals, and some lacy lingerie. Rory gave Amanda some yellow patterned silk he had brought back from Vietnam, and she made a short negligee trimmed in lace and tied with yellow ribbons.

The package containing Amanda's finished dress arrived, and Amanda tried it on. It fit perfectly! Included were lace mitts, trimmed in green silk. Also in the package from her mother were baby doll pajamas—filmy and elaborately embroidered. Her trousseau was complete! She shopped with Rory when he chose a dark blue suit, a white dress shirt, a tie in shades of blue, and new black dress shoes.

As they were leaving the store, Rory stopped.

"Do you need to get anything else? Lingerie or anything? Do you have a new nightgown?" he asked. His face turned slightly pink, and Amanda hid a smile.

"Yes, I think I have everything. Mama sent me a nightgown," she answered.

"Your *mother* bought your nightgown?" he asked, in amazement.

Amanda was amused. She looked at him innocently, "Yes, she did. Is anything wrong?"

Rory stared at her a moment. "No, nothing's wrong."

Amanda bit her lip to keep from giggling. He thinks it will be a granny gown or something. Will he be surprised!

Amanda borrowed Debbie's wedding veil, and a friend at work gave her a little package containing a tiny blue sachet and a new penny. She would put one in each shoe.

David and Debbie were asked to be best man and matron-of-honor. Elizabeth would be the flower girl. Matthew and Joshua would usher, along with Ed. Amanda and Rory spoke with the church organist and planned the music: traditional processional and recessional.

Catherine and Patricia would make the wedding cake. The

reception would be at Amanda's house immediately after the wedding, and would include family and friends. Only the family would attend the wedding.

Rory's father, Ron, called Rory and told him he would fly in the day before the wedding, but his wife would be unable to come. Rory was so pleased that his father would be there. He hadn't seen him in some time, and no one else in his family could attend.

Amanda and Rory ordered the flowers together. She wanted white daisies with yellow centers in a posy-style bouquet. Rory would have a white carnation, as would James, Rory's father, David, Matthew, and Joshua. Debbie and Catherine would have yellow sweet pea corsages, and Elizabeth would have a basket of yellow and white petals to strew in the aisle. They ordered two small baskets of mixed spring flowers in yellow and white for either side of the altar.

Elizabeth's dress took only three evenings to make. Then Amanda bought little white pumps and white tights to go with the dress. She also bought sports jackets and trousers for Matthew and Joshua—suits were too expensive and not very practical, she decided.

On the Saturday before the wedding, Rory borrowed a pickup and they moved most of Rory's furniture to Amanda's house. The living room was crowded, but the extra seating was welcomed. Some items were stored in the basement and two beds were set up there, in one end, for family visits. They also moved most of Rory's clothes. Amanda had made half of the closet available, and emptied drawers in the dresser and the chest. They put his things away together, between shy hugs. The long months were almost over.

Amanda planned the menu for the reception (about 25-30 guests were expected), and did her shopping Monday evening. She would make little cream puffs and fill them with chicken salad, chicken liver paté, tiny meat balls, and baked cheese balls. That, with mints, nuts, fruit punch, and wine punch would suffice. She had previously purchased the nicest paper plates she could find. There were too many guests to use her china. She had also purchased napkins in a wedding theme at the stationery store. At the last moment, she uncharacteristically added two cans of caviar to her shopping cart, marveling at her extravagance. She bought rosé wine for punch. Rory would take care of the champagne.

Her hair appointment was for 8:00 Friday morning, at a shop on the base. She asked for time off for that and for Friday afternoon. The major urged her to take the entire day off, but she felt she could not afford that.

Tuesday and Wednesday evening were spent cooking and baking. Rory came late in the evening after class on both days, to view her labors before they were wrapped and stored in the freezer compartment. All had his full approval, except the paté. Her refrigerator bulged with olives, punch makings, and the caviar. She made a note to put toast triangles on the "to-do" list for Catherine and the other members of her family, who would preside at the reception. Matthew and Joshua were sent to find the punch bowl, in a box stored in the basement. Amanda had located a smaller punch bowl among Rory's things, and it would serve for the fruit punch. She made two ice rings in molds, with strawberries embedded in the ice. She washed platters and little glass bowls for the mints and nuts. Elizabeth polished silverware with energy. Tinker had no definite task, and on his own initiative, got underfoot as only he could. Rory chose the music albums they would play on the stereo. Ed and Matthew would be taking photographs.

Wednesday evening, Rory and Amanda sat at the table after the children were in bed, poring over her lists, hoping nothing had been forgotten. They yawned, and couldn't stop yawning, although they had consumed numerous cups of coffee.

In exasperation, Rory exclaimed, "Amanda, I thought we agreed on a small wedding. It's gotten out of hand!"

Amanda looked up from her stack of lists. Rory's brow was creased in a frown and his hair stuck out every which way. A smile touched her lips, only to fade as she wondered what her hair looked like.

"We should have eloped," Rory muttered.

Amanda giggled a few moments, then burst into tears. Rory pulled her to her feet and held her against his chest, telling her everything would be fine, and at length, she was quiet.

"Are you okay, now?" Rory asked, holding her away from him a few inches. She nodded and he wiped her tears with his handkerchief.

"You get some sleep, and I'll see you tomorrow. You're worn out." He kissed the top of her head and left.

Amanda turned out lights, brushed her teeth, dropped her clothes on a chair, and fell into bed. "Jesus, please let me not forget anything important," she prayed and fell asleep.

Catherine, James, Sue, and Jeanette were at the house when Amanda got home Thursday afternoon. The rest of the family would arrive on Friday. Catherine looked at Amanda, hugged her and sent her to her room for a nap. Amanda meekly obeyed, and Catherine closed her bedroom door. The children stood wide-eyed, watching their mother obey Grandma.

When Amanda woke an hour later, she felt refreshed. She splashed water on her face and joined the others in the living room. The rehearsal would be at seven. Rory called. He had picked up his father at the airport. They were to stay overnight at a motel and get reacquainted. He told Amanda he would see her in a while at the church.

Catherine set out the children's clothes while Amanda packed her bag. Then they went over the recipes, table setting, plates, platters, and bowls to be used. They discussed how to keep hot food hot, etc. Catherine had brought a lace tablecloth and Amanda planned to use her bridal bouquet for a centerpiece, and throw it before leaving.

Amanda, her parents, her children, and Sue and Jeanette arrived at the church at 6:25 for rehearsal. Rory arrived a few minutes later with his father, Ron. Rory immediately introduced Amanda to Ron, and he gave her a big smile and a hug. He was Rory's height and slender. His hair was dark, but Amanda could see the resemblance in father and son—same hairline, same twinkle in the eyes, though Ron's were darker. Amanda sat in a left-hand pew, a few rows back from the altar of the church, and Ron sat with her. She was not allowed to participate in the rehearsal, but she listened intently to the minister.

First, he explained the ushers' duties to Matthew and Joshua. Ed was not there, but he had ushered at several weddings and would have no problem with the small attendance at this one. Then the organist began playing prelude music, and the wedding party took their places, with Sue, shyly, taking Amanda's part.

It seemed unreal to Amanda, and in a sense it was, but she couldn't juxtapose what she was watching onto the actual ceremony that would take place tomorrow. She had waited so long, had planned every detail, and now, she could not visualize herself walking down this aisle. She tried to focus on all the things she would be expected to do—walk slowly, repeat her vows, kneel, hand her bouquet to Debbie, put the ring on Rory's finger—she must not forget the ring! It was all jumbled up in her mind. *I'll never get through this*, she thought. Her hands were shaking and she clasped them tightly together in her lap. Ron placed a hand over hers, and gave them a quick squeeze. She turned and smiled a shaky, but grateful smile. By this time tomorrow, all the waiting, the anxious moments, all will be over—and she would be Rory's wife! Rory would be her husband! *It's just a dream, I'll wake up soon....*

Suddenly Rory was beside her. What was he saying? He took her arm and helped her to her feet.

"Are you ready? We can go to dinner now," he asked, looking at her curiously.

Of course, they were all to have dinner! Amanda mentally shook herself out of her reverie and smiled at Rory. "Ready!" she said, "I'm starved!"

They had reservations at a family restaurant and ate at one long table in a small conference room. It was a festive party. Amanda and Rory accepted the mild ribbing with aplomb.

Rory gave Amanda a quick kiss outside the restaurant and drove away with Ron. David and Debbie put their girls in the car and left for home, and everyone else went to Amanda's, where they soon retired. Tomorrow would be a busy and exciting day.

"Father, I am so tired," Amanda prayed, as she lay on her bed, "please let everything get done. Thank You for Mama, and the others, and all their help. I am nervous, and I can't seem to concentrate very well. What it is, Lord, is that I'm scared silly. Why? I know Rory loves me, and I love him. I know You are with us. Rory and the children are truly building a relationship. It's foolish of me, but it's true. I am so happy, but I'm scared. I know You did not give me a spirit of fear, so please take it away. And let me do everything well tomorrow. Please be there at the ceremony. Join us together with Your love. Amen."

29

Sing unto him a new song

(Psalm 33:3)

At eight o'clock, Amanda was at the hair dresser's. As the young woman shampooed her hair and chatted, Amanda answered her questions and tried to relax as her head was massaged, but her thoughts were on last night's rehearsal, and the coming hours. She watched the mirror image as curlers began to sprout all over her head, and then she was under the hot dryer. Soon the curlers were being removed and skillful hands brushed and combed dark hair that hung in soft waves below the shoulders. The sides were swept up and pinned in little curls on top of the head. Feathery bangs swept over the brow. This image didn't resemble the casual hairdo Amanda favored. And that white face—it surely wasn't hers. She had never needed coloring on her cheeks—they were naturally pink. This was a stranger in the mirror.

"What do you think? Do you like it?" the hairdresser asked.

"It's beautiful. Yes, I like it," Amanda answered automatically, and smiled. But it was difficult to associate that glamorous looking hair-do with herself.

She walked the short distance to work and was greeted with words of approval. By 10:30, they convinced her to go home, telling her she needed time to relax. They ushered her out the door with smiles and promises to see her at the reception.

At home, there was a flurry of activity—last-minute dusting and wiping, Catherine and Patricia were putting the cake together. It had been transported in its several layers. Kate and Sue were constructing hors d'oeuvres. After greetings, hugs, and admiring Amanda's hair, they returned to their tasks. She walked toward the kitchen to pitch in and was gently but firmly told she was not needed, and to go take a nap. Someone would do her nails in an hour or so, and would wake her. Everything, she was told, was under control.

Amanda, slightly bewildered, meekly obeyed. She lay on top of the spread, carefully arranging her hair, and, to her later surprise, dozed off.

She was wakened. Kate did her nails, she had a leisurely bath, and was putting on her make-up when she heard a commotion at the back door. She started down the hall, hearing Rory's voice, and was stopped by Catherine. Rory was arguing with Patricia, who refused to let him in.

"You can't see her on your wedding day, not until the ceremony."

"I just want to see her for a minute," Rory pleaded.

"No. It's bad luck. I'll give her a message."

"I don't have a message. I want to *see* her."

"Rory! You must not see her until she comes down the aisle. I'm sorry," said Patricia, firmly.

"She's all right, isn't she?"

"Of course, she's all right! She's getting ready. You should go get ready, too. It's less than two hours until the wedding. Amanda has to go to the church soon."

Amanda opened her mouth to speak, but Catherine squeezed her arm and shook her head. "Be quiet," she said, smiling. "You'll see each other soon enough." Amanda heard the back door close, and went back to her bedroom.

Debbie arrived a short while later to take Amanda to the church where she would finish dressing. The dressing room at the church included a small bathroom and a huge mirror.

Amanda removed her slacks and shirt, as Debbie laid out the bridal clothes. Suddenly Amanda began shaking. The shoes she was holding in one hand clattered to the floor. Her breathing quickened into gasps for air. Debbie pushed her into a chair.

"Take deep breaths, Amanda. Deeper!" Debbie commanded. She brought dampened paper towels and pressed them at the back of Amanda's neck.

In a few minutes, Amanda's breathing returned to near normal. Her face was blotched red and white.

"Do you feel better now? You scared the daylights out of me! That's the worst case of nerves I've ever seen!"

"I don't know what came over me!" exclaimed Amanda, in a shaky voice. She glanced in the mirror. Horrified, her hands went to her face. "Look at me, I look awful!"

"You'll be fine in a few minutes. Just relax a bit. Here, hold this wet towel on your face. We may have to redo some of your make-up."

Amanda's hands went to her forehead. "Oh, my head aches."

"Do you have aspirin in your purse? No, you didn't bring it, did you? I don't have any." Debbie rummaged in her own bag.

"What I want is a cigarette, Debbie. I'm sorry, but I really do. I didn't bring any with me."

"I'll go find some. Can you start getting dressed? I'll be right back."

Amanda nodded and picked up her panty hose. Debbie returned in a few minutes, brandishing a packet of cigarettes.

"Compliments of your new father-in-law," she said, smiling.

"Father-in-law! He probably thinks I'm a nut case! I think so, too!" She lit a cigarette with shaky hands and sat quietly for a minute or two. *Father, I am so ashamed of myself,* she prayed. *Please forgive me. I have been so busy the last few days, I haven't talked to You like I should have. And now, I am so nervous and afraid. Please take that away, Jesus. I love Rory and I want to be his wife more than anything on this earth. You know my heart. You know that is true. Please help me. I want to enjoy this ceremony. I want to remember it with joy. Please help me. Thank You. Amen.*

"We need to hurry, Amanda. It's getting late," Debbie reminded her.

Amanda looked at her watch. "Oh, dear, it *is* late." She went to the bathroom, rinsed her mouth, gently patted her face with her fingers, and added more lipstick to her lips. When she came out, Debbie was holding her dress up for Amanda to slip on. Then her shoes, and finally she sat as Debbie arranged the veil over her curls.

"Stand up and let's have a look," said Debbie. Amanda obeyed, turning slowly in a full circle. Debbie was smiling, "Beautiful! You have the penny in your shoe? The blue garter?" Amanda nodded, and Debbie went on, "I have Rory's ring." She opened the door to listen to the music.

Ed slipped into view and beckoned to Debbie. "We must go now. Are you ready?" she asked.

Amanda gave her a tentative smile. "I'm ready. I'm scared silly, but I'm ready."

Debbie squeezed her arm. "You look absolutely gorgeous!" she said and walked down the short hall.

Catherine and James, and Elizabeth were waiting in the anteroom at the back of the sanctuary. Catherine gave her an encouraging smile and a hug and left with Matthew, who took her arm to escort her to her seat. Joshua gave James an embarrassed grin and held out his arm. James winked at him and they stepped out behind Catherine and Matthew.

Elizabeth held her basket out to her side, and when Matthew

and Joshua returned, Debbie motioned to her to begin her slow walk down the aisle, and whispered, "Don't forget to drop the flower petals." Elizabeth put one hand into the basket and picked up a few petals, and moved to the door. Debbie watched and after Elizabeth had made a dozen steps or so, she followed, giving Amanda a reassuring smile over her shoulder. The music changed.

Amanda gripped her bouquet tightly, pasted a smile on her face and stepped out, slowly. Her glance swept down the aisle as she forced one foot in front of the other. Everyone was looking at her, expectantly, smiling. There was Elizabeth, just turning to the side of the altar, Debbie halfway down the aisle; the minister stood, his arms behind him. Another step. "Please Jesus, be here with me." David stood at the far side, and Rory, looking very handsome, stood next to the minister. Step. Step. Her eyes returned to Rory—Rory, who had stolen her heart in an instant, and in return, had given her life meaning. He was smiling at her; and she smiled, too, behind her veil. "Thank You, Thank You!" Her steps quickened, became firm. Rory was waiting for her.

Amanda's New Song is based on actual events. All names of characters have been changed. Most real of all is Amanda's Friend, who had and has an active part in her life. He wants to be your Friend as well. If you have not met Him, you can do so now. He is waiting for you to invite Him in. Just pray this prayer from your heart:

Lord Jesus, I want to know You; I want You to be my Friend. I believe You are the Son of the Living God, that You came to earth as a baby, and died on the cross for my sins. I believe You have the power to forgive my sins and I ask You to do that now. Jesus, I have sinned and I ask You, from my heart, to please wash my sins away, and adopt me as Your child.

Thank You, Jesus, for saving me. I now acknowledge You as my Savior and Redeemer, and I know Your Spirit now lives in my heart. Amen.

If you prayed from your heart, you have just made the most important decision of your life. Congratulations! God's angels are rejoicing and God has written your name in His Book of Life. You can record your rebirth by writing your name, and the day and hour in which you received eternal life.

Name	*Date*	*Hour*

1

Endnotes

[1] Teasdale, Sara. *Night.*

[2] Shipman, Herbert. *No Thoroughfare.*